Primal Surrender

THE SURRENDER SERIES III

By: Lori King

BLURB

Brothers Mack and Ryker Thompson know the pain of failure intimately having recently fallen from the heights of success. One a former football star, and the other a master at his artistic craft, they couldn't be more different from each other. Mack hides behind anonymity in order to cover up his pain, while Ryker figures it doesn't matter if the glass is half-full or half-empty as long as there's a bartender refilling it all will be well. Broken and haunted by the mistakes of their past, neither expected to find a ray of sunshine in the clouds of their pity party.

Claudia Schmidt, is the only daughter of a real estate tycoon that has a plan for turning the small town of Stone River into a suburb of Austin, Texas. When she is sent in to replace the project manager, and convince the town of the necessity of the project, she finds herself falling in love with the town, and the Thompson brothers.

Although ménage relationships aren't foreign to Mack and Ryker, neither one intends on living one, so how can they decide who gets the girl? And what if the girl wants all or nothing? Welcome back to Stone River...

(M/F/M/M/M Ménage, public exhibition, consensual BDSM, bondage, spanking, HEA, *There is no touching or titillation between siblings.*)

DEDICATION

For my parents;
Who taught me that family and love are more important than anything else.
Thank you.
I hope to always Live, Laugh, and Love like today is my only chance,
-Lori

ACKNOWLEDGEMENTS:

Four very special ladies helped me creatively on this story:
Diana Merrit who helped create Cormac "Mack" Thompson last summer
when I was writing Weekend Surrender.
Trixie Shellbomb who won the opportunity to help me create the character
Ryker Thompson.
Rhoda Siller who suggested the name Saddle-Up Leatherworks.
And Trish Bowers who suggested the name Tan Your Hyde Leatherworks.
Thank you for your assistance, ladies!

CHAPTER ONE

"I just don't get it. Why the hell would anyone want to share his wife with his brother?"

Mack Thompson grimaced at his brother, Ryker's, rude question while watching the bride kiss each of her three grooms. Zoey Carson—now Keegan—was best friends with Rachel Brooks. The pair were two of the hottest women in town, and at one time Mack had considered asking Zoey out. But the Keegan brothers beat him to the punch, snapping her up before he had the chance. Just like the Brooks boys had captivated Rachel and put a baby in her belly and a ring on her finger in the blink of an eye. It seemed like everyone around them was finding their happily-ever-after, while Mack and Ryker were alone. Forced to endure each other's company, while crammed into the tiny cabin on the east edge of Brooks Pastures horse ranch.

Mack surveyed the glowing bride in her white wedding gown. With her stunning blue eyes and long dark hair, she reminded him of a fairy princess. He had to admit she looked happier than he had ever seen her and the three grooms looked like love-struck puppy dogs. Even the stoic Tanner Keegan grinned from ear to ear as he moved to her side and tugged her against him. The sweet way she relaxed into his grip had Mack's nuts tingling in his jeans, causing him to fidget in his seat.

He didn't understand why anyone would want to share their woman either. It went against everything he knew, but he couldn't deny their happiness. The contentment of his bosses and new friends with their relationships was remarkable. Just spending time with them left a ball of envy burning in his gut, but he would support them any way possible. No matter what his own feelings were.

"Because they all three love her. It wouldn't have been fair to make her choose and leave two of them left with broken hearts," Mack responded, thinking the argument was as logical as any.

Ryker shook his head in wonder. "I guess, I figured it shouldn't have gotten to the point that she was in love with all three. If one of them called dibs the other two should have backed off. That's what you and I would do."

Mack shrugged feeling the tag in the back of his gray Henley scratch across his back as he did. He hated dressing up. It seemed like a waste of time to put on clothes you didn't like just to make someone else happy. He was a whole lot more comfortable in blue jeans, a t-shirt, and his black motorcycle boots. Tucking his heels underneath the rickety wooden chair he sat in, he tried to hide his too tight and too shiny dress shoes. He had purchased them for the Brooks wedding a year ago. That was the last time he put the whole getup on, and if he was lucky this would be the last time he had to do it for a long while.

"Mack, Ryker, thank you guys so much for coming. I know it's Christmas Eve, so it means a lot that you were willing to come spend it with us." Zoey's warm sapphire gaze encompassed the two brothers and they both rose to accept a hug from her.

"We wouldn't miss it for the world. I had to see another coup against the male population of Texas with my own eyes." Ryker's smart mouth was going to be the death of him. Mack shot him a nasty glare over Zoey's head.

"Oh no, this wasn't some sort of hostile takeover, they begged me to marry them. On bended knee, no less!" Zoey said with a laugh.

Ryker's smile widened, "Yes, but what did you do to bring them to their knees, sunshine? Because something tells me you used a few of your feminine wiles on them."

"Ignore him, Zoey. He's just jaded and jealous of your happiness. While I am just happy you softened up Tanner's mean temper a little bit," Mack said, hoping to shift the pretty bride away from his brother's negativity.

Mack didn't blame Ryk for his depression. It just irked him. Lately it had been getting harder and harder to let his brother's vile mouth spew without shoving a fist into his teeth to knock the arrogance out of him. Ryker Thompson had been a starting running back for three different pro football teams in the ten years since college. For years his life seemed damn near perfect, until he reinjured his shoulder and it put him out of the game for good. At first, the doctors thought surgery and physical therapy might get him back on the field. After the surgery their prognosis changed. The torn ligaments and muscles wouldn't ever be up to the physical pressure of football tackles, so his team cut him loose.

As if that blow wasn't bad enough emotionally, after surgery, Ryk found out his female business manager had seduced his male accountant and the two had left him high and dry. They disappeared with all the money he had. As a result, he had a mansion and three sports cars he couldn't pay for. The ongoing search for the pair by authorities hadn't turned up much yet. They had boarded a plane for the Cayman's and vanished. He had to make the tough decision to sell his home and vehicles, so he would have money to live on. Moving in with Mack while he recovered from surgery became a necessity. For the last four months the two brothers had been stepping on each other's toes as Ryk tried to figure out what to do next.

"Well I can't say that was easy!" Zoey giggled as her eyes sought out her husband. It was like their souls connected when their eyes met, and Mack felt like a pervert for viewing the intimacy first hand. "But, he was worth it. Are you guys staying for dinner?"

Before Mack could respond, Ryk shook his head, "No. My shoulder's bothering me, so we're going to head out."

The flash of disappointment on Zoey's face sent rage rushing through his chest. Mack had to force his fists into his pockets to keep from teaching his little brother some respect. Ryker's sullen nastiness boiled down to jealousy, but it was sure getting old.

"Thank you for the invite, Zoey, but I had better get the old man home. I don't want him to keel over on me. Congratulations on your big day. You look beautiful." Mack pressed a kiss to her cheek, and she gave him a warm smile.

"Thank you, Mack. And thank you again for helping with the ranch while we go to Cabo next weekend. I'm sure the new ranch hands could have managed, but Tanner will feel better knowing you're supervising." As if his name summoned him, Tanner stepped up behind his wife, and bent low to nuzzle her neck.

"She's right. It does make it easier for me to leave. You know I haven't been on a vacation since I took over the ranch?" Tanner looked thoughtful, "I'm looking forward to seeing my new wife in a bikini."

Zoey snorted, "Like you haven't seen that before? We live in Texas not Canada. I wear a bikini every time we go camping."

"Yeah, but now you're our wife," Dalton appeared on her other side and captured her hand, bringing it to his lips for a kiss. "We don't have to apologize for our lecherous thoughts about you anymore."

"You know I don't recall you ever apologizing for them before, Mr. Keegan," Zoey answered. Her head fell back against Tanner's shoulder, and she laced her fingers through Dalton's. They were the picture of happiness, so beautiful it was painful to look at.

Ryker's anxious fidgeting drew Mack's attention and he rushed to say his goodbyes and herd his brother home. He wasn't going to chance Ryk saying anything that would spoil the Keegan family's joy. From the stories Mack had heard, those four deserved every beautiful moment they could get.

It was only a few minutes before Mack was parking his big blue Dodge Ram in front of the foreman's cabin on Brooks Pastures land. Ryk was out of the vehicle and pushing through the front door before Mack had a chance to even shove his keys in his pocket. Annoyance rippled through him. This was getting ridiculous.

Ryk spent ninety percent of his time sitting in the house on his laptop looking at sports reports or watching football. His moping was getting redundant and Mack was over it. Seeing him be so callous toward Zoey's blissful happiness was the last straw.

Slamming the door open, he stood between Ryk and the oversized television, feet braced, and arms crossed. "What the hell is your problem?"

Ryker sputtered for a minute. He cursed at him for blocking his view of yet another sports recap about some game that happened weeks ago, but Mack refused to budge.

"Ryk, it's Christmas Eve, and it's Zoey's wedding day. You couldn't even summon up a little decency to congratulate her like a normal human being. What the fuck is your problem?"

Fury broke over Ryker's face and he launched himself out of the easy chair tackling Mack to the ground. Pain burned through Mack's jaw when Ryk's fist planted into it. He didn't hesitate to take the swings he had been itching for earlier. Rolling on the living room floor, the two exchanged punches, jabs, and kicks until they were both in pain and out of breath. Their anger forced out of them via their fists. Glaring at his brother in silence, Mack pressed the hem of his shirt to his split lip and waited.

"I don't want to be happy for anyone. I don't want anyone to be happy at all. I'm not happy. Why the hell should they get to live in some sort of group sex utopia, while I'm stuck jerking off in the shower and sharing a one bedroom shack with my older brother?" The words dripped off Ryk's tongue like acid, burning through Mack's heart. Ryk was clearly more affected by his situation than even his brother had realized.

"Fuck, Ryk. Wishing everyone else a shitty life just because you've had some hurdles—"

"Hurdles? Is that what it's called? Fuck that! I was a star, damn it. I made more money in ten years than you will ever see in a lifetime, and it's all gone. Gone because of one stupid shift to the left when I should have gone right. Gone because I trusted a fucking woman to handle my business. Instead of being professional, her pussy stole every penny I've got, and any chance I had at a decent future." Ryker shoved to his feet and stomped toward the kitchen. Mack was a little slower to rise, feeling the pull in his left side that indicated he had a bruised rib. Ryk didn't look much better, his nose was already swollen to twice its normal size, and blood speckled his shirt. They didn't fight often, but when they did it was usually bloody.

"You know what? You are a selfish asswipe. It was their wedding day, fuckwad. You can't see past your own problems for two hours so they could enjoy their special day. I get it. You've lost everything, but you still have the use of your shoulder. Those two thieves will get caught—"

"And I'll get my money back? Yeah, right. Let me explain how the real world works, big brother, even if the law catches up to them, my money is long gone. I'm flat broke, and I can't even go back to the job I love and start over." Ryker slammed two bags of ice on the counter. Mack gave him a begrudging nod of thanks when he slid one across to him.

"So you can't play ball, big fucking deal. You have a hell of a lot more talent than you give yourself credit for. You trusted the wrong person to handle your money, but you had money to begin with because you have a good head for business. Everyone screws up, Ryk, stop acting like a girl. Man up or pack your shit because I won't risk you poisoning the people I care about with your nasty attitude."

Ryker glared at him, but Mack refused to back down. "You can't tell me you're happy with your life. Two years ago you were Cormac Thompson, owner and operator of Saddle-Up Leather. One of the biggest and best leather working businesses in Texas. Now you're just, Mack the farmhand. Can you say you're content being the foreman on a horse ranch now?"

"No." Mack shook his head, "No, I'm not happy with that. I want more for my life, but I can't change what happened in the past. I didn't have your head for business, and I managed to run mine into the ground when everyone lost their shit in the recession. I fought like hell to keep it together for almost four years before I let the business go under. I'm lucky to have friends like Parker Brooks and his brothers who were willing to lend me a hand and give me a job."

"As a ranch hand," Ryker sneered, and Mack had to work to control his temper.

"Yes, as a foreman on a horse ranch. One of the best goddamn ranches in the world, and I work for some great people. I won't be here forever, and neither will you, but I will put one hundred percent in while I am. I'd rather be known for my strengths than my weaknesses. You need to make a decision, Ryk. Are you going to waste away in that recliner moping about the glories that should have been yours? Or are you going to grow a pair of balls and create a new set of plans for yourself?"

With that, Mack spun on his heel and stormed out of the kitchen. In three large steps he was in his bedroom where he was able to slam the door behind him soothing some of the rage and pain he felt for his brother. He understood what Ryker was going through. Falling from the top to the bottom hurt more than a person could bear sometimes. But it didn't mean a man couldn't climb back up if he wanted to. It was a matter of pride, and right now, he wasn't sure Ryker had any.

CHAPTER TWO

Six months later…

The Garden Hut's particular scent burned Mack's nostrils every time he entered the small store. It came from selling everything from garden gnomes and pesticides, to manure, and it was unique to the establishment. Today the building seemed to be unusually empty. Mack couldn't see anyone in the store, other than the young man who was sitting behind the cash register with a skate boarding magazine in his hands and ear buds in his ears. The teenager looked up and gave him a nod, but didn't seem inclined to move from his seat, so Mack just nodded back as he walked by.

He had just found what he came in for when he heard a raspy voice mumbling in the next aisle. The person sounded vexed and Mack couldn't resist a peek to see what the trouble was. Standing in front of a display of plant pesticides was a beautiful curvy woman with a mane of blonde curls and lush red lips that were pursed in frustration. She was wearing a blazer and slim skirt that ended a few inches above her knees, and she had a heavy looking purse slung over one shoulder. Her hands were planted on her ample hips while she tapped one high-heeled shoe with the rhythm of her thoughts. Those shoes were death defyingly high, and capped off the sexiest pair of legs he had ever seen. It was a miracle the zipper on his jeans held. When she noticed him standing there, she turned and her lips curved up a in a small smile. Mack felt like he swallowed his tongue.

"Hi." Her voice was rough and husky, not particularly feminine, but seductively intriguing anyway. It suited her. So did her tawny hazel eyes. More of a cappuccino color than green, but the flecks of green dotting them were unmistakable. With that mane of golden hair and her blonde fringe of eyelashes she reminded him of a female lion.

"Hi. Were you having trouble finding something?" He cursed himself for fumbling in front of the beautiful bombshell, and her eyes sparkled with amusement.

"Do you work here?"

Mack shook his head, and gestured to the bag of zip ties he was holding. "No, I'm a customer. I just heard you talking to yourself and—"

His words were cut off when she took a step closer and peered at the package he held. She smelled of cocoa butter and vanilla. It was a heady combination for a man who normally spent his time surrounded by horses and leather.

"One hundred and twenty pound rated zip ties. You must be tying up something big," she said, cocking her head to one side and running her gaze from the top of his curly blonde hair to the toes of his scuffed up motorcycle boots.

Mack felt the pink warmth crawling up his cheeks, and it was clear by her widening smile she saw it. He averted his gaze to the package in his hand cursing his pale skin, and forced his shoulders back. Somehow she had made him forget himself, and that wasn't acceptable at all. "It's for securing temporary horse corrals. I work on a horse ranch."

She nodded, and adjusted her bag. "Ah, I see. Well, Mr.—"

Her voice drifted off, and Mack found himself lost in the shifting colors of her eyes again. It wasn't until she cleared her throat that he realized she was waiting for him to fill in the blank.

"Thompson. Mack Thompson."

"Mr. Thompson, I am trying to figure out which of these bottles will get rid of the teeny tiny little green bugs I found on my rose bushes last night. Would you happen to know?"

Mack stared at her while imagining her in a garden surrounded by blooming roses, with absolutely nothing covering her delicious curves from his view. She would be Eve and he would be happy to play her Adam.

Giving himself a mental shake, he turned to the bottles on the shelf, "It sounds like aphids, so you're going to want something that kills the bugs, but if you aren't treating your garden regularly to prevent them they will just come back. You have to be on your game with pests, or they will control everything before you know it."

He reached for a bottle and turned to hand it to her, surprised to find her looking at him with amused curiosity on her face. "Oh, I don't let too many things gain the upper hand in my life. I'll have those bugs surrendering in no time."

A ripple of lust heated him from his belly to his balls at the mere mention of surrendering. What would it be like to surrender to this luscious Aphrodite? He could picture her in thigh high boots, riding his cock and screaming for him to give her more. When the lust cleared from his eyes, he shifted awkwardly and wondered if he had somehow given his own secrets away, but the woman didn't let on if that was the case.

"Well that should do it unless you have a really large garden and then you'll want to get a sprayer and the concentrated kind."

She shook her head, and held the bottle against her breasts. And amazing breasts they were. They would overflow his hands, and he would guess there were large nipples on their tips that would taste delicious.

"So tell me, Mr. Thompson, how does a rancher know about rose bushes?"

Mack grimaced as he followed her down the aisle and back toward the cash register. "My mama has a rose garden. I've spent my share of time on my knees in one, pulling weeds."

She flashed him a wide smile before handing the teenager some cash and collecting her bag. "Lucky for me. Thank you for your expertise. I'd better get home and start battling the bugs immediately."

With that she was out the door with a friendly wave and a wink. Mack was left standing at the counter feeling like the earth had just been ripped out from under his feet. The woman was gorgeous, outgoing, and flirty—and he hadn't even managed to get her name. He must be some kind of stupid.

"That will be seventeen fifty."

The teen's voice pierced through Mack's brain and he grunted at him while passing him the money. "You wouldn't happen to know that woman's name would you, kid?"

The boy's lip and eyebrow rose simultaneously signaling his confusion, and Mack took mercy on him. "Yeah, never mind. I'll find out myself."

Snatching up the zip ties, he pushed his way out the door, relieved to see a waterfall of blonde curls climbing into a cherry red Mercedes Benz. Taking a chance he stepped off the sidewalk and directly into the path of her car so she couldn't back out of the stall without running him down. One of her perfectly sculpted eyebrows rose until it was lost under the curl of her bangs, and she pursed her lips as she rolled down the window.

"Do you mind?" Annoyance laced her tone, but her body language was still relaxed, so he gave her his most charming smile.

"I didn't get your name."

Her hazel eyes widened minutely, and a tiny smile played at the corners of her mouth. "Why do you need it?"

Lowering his body so he was crouched next to the luxurious vehicle, he considered that perhaps this woman was out of his league. Her clothes were high end, her car was top of the line, and if he wasn't mistaken the highlights in her blonde hair were professionally done. So it stood to reason she was privileged enough to take insult from his low class flirtations. Instead of deterring him, the challenge turned him on, and he braced his forearms on her window.

"I like to know a woman's name before I ask her out."

Her laughter was husky like her voice and it stroked through him like a caress on his soul, pressing a button inside of him that was unlikely to ever reset. "Are all ranchers so forward?"

Mack shrugged, "I figure if you turn me down it will be your loss. I'm a hell of a two stepper, Miss…"

His words drifted off into heavy silence. The blonde beauty held his gaze for several tense breaths before she snorted and rolled her eyes. "I'm Claudia, Claudia Schmidt." She stared at him looking somewhat apprehensive, and he cocked his head as he wondered where he had heard the name before. "Schmidt as in Schmidt Properties."

It all clicked and he barely managed to keep from groaning out loud. "Ah, the developer that's buying up half of Stone River to build suburbs for Austin's elite. Right?"

He knew the moment the words left his lips it was the wrong thing to say. Her eyes grew hard and her jaw muscle twitched as she clenched her teeth. The interest he had seen was clearly shelved for the day, as she withdrew further into her car and placed her finger over the button for the window. "Yes, that Schmidt. Now, if you'll excuse me, Mr. Thompson I need to get going."

"I'm sorry. I didn't mean it the way it sounded." Mack left his hand on the window frame so she wouldn't shut it and essentially shut him out.

"Oh, you didn't mean to imply I'm some kind of rich bitch who's here to push poor people out into the cold so my kind of people can build mini-mansions on the land their families have owned for decades? Really? So how exactly did you mean it, Mr. Thompson?"

She was gorgeous when she was mad. Her hazel eyes darkened into a cappuccino color flecked with green fire, and her creamy white skin flushed pink as her blood pressure rose. He could imagine her in a different place altogether all rosy pink with passion and his cock suddenly throbbed in his jeans. Tearing his gaze away from her pursed lips, he tried to look contrite as her words sunk into his brain. "Look, I see now that work is a sensitive subject for you—"

"Goodbye, Mr. Thompson." She pressed down on the button and the window began to close, carrying his hand with it.

"Just wait a damn minute!" Frustration made his voice sharper than he intended, but she paused in her motion and glared at him impatiently.

"First of all, my name is Mack, not Mr. Thompson; second, I don't care if you're a member of the royal family here to start the second revolution, I still want to take you out. And third, your thin skin isn't going to help you make friends in this part of Texas, Ms. Schmidt. Cowboys aren't known for their tact, and as you just witnessed, I personally have a bad habit of putting my foot in my mouth."

He was pleased when she removed her hand from the window switch. The window was still halfway up, but it wasn't shutting any further, and he took it as a good sign.

"Now that we've cleared the air, I'll get back to the point. I want to take you dancing tonight at Robin's. I can't promise you wine and roses here in Stone River, but I can promise a cold beer, good food, great music, and I swear I won't step on your toes. What do you say?"

Her lip twitched like she was fighting to hold back a smile, "I say you're out of your mind. You just insulted me and now you want me to go out on a date with you."

Mack shrugged and grinned, "Maybe a little, but I figure you owe me."

"I owe you?" She sounded haughty, but the husky tone of her laughter took any steam out of her annoyance for him. "Pray tell, how do you figure I owe you?"

"Well I did save you a lot of trouble by giving you gardening advice. Do you know how quick aphids will kill off a rose garden? The way I see it you owe me a beer to say thanks; however, I prefer to just take you out tonight and call us even."

~ ~ ~

Claudia stared at the big man outside her car window in astonished fascination. Somehow, she had gone from intrigued, to irritated, and back to intrigued in less than two minutes. How was that possible?

She had to give him credit for his creativity and his persistence. Not many people could argue her into a corner, and some of the best had tried. Instead of the requisite cowboy hat, his blonde hair curled out from under a red bandana. It was a stark frame for his wide face and crystal clear blue eyes. They were so light in color they almost looked gray in the bright sunshine, and she imagined staring into the shifting colors of his irises for hours without growing bored. When his smile stretched wider, highlighting the pair of deep dimples in his cheeks, she sighed heavily.

"Fine. One beer tonight at Robin's, I'll meet you there."

His smile dimmed a fraction, "Meet me there? I would prefer to pick you up, but if it will make you more comfortable—"

"Take it or leave it Mr. Thomp—Mack." His name on her lips felt right, and her heart flip-flopped when his nostrils flared and a smug look of satisfaction crossed his face.

"I'll take it, Claudia. Eight o'clock, don't be late." Mack tapped his hand against her car door, and stood placing a huge denim covered bulge right in her line of sight. She swallowed hard as her mind ran screaming off into wild fantasies of what the big man had tucked behind his zipper and how he might use it on her. Before she could formulate a response, he had turned around giving her an unobstructed view of his equally tantalizing backside, swaggering across the parking lot to a huge blue truck.

Throwing her car into gear, she backed out of the parking stall a little too fast and had to resist flooring it and peeling out of the lot. On her way past, Mack gave her a wink and a wave that both delighted and irritated her.

What was she thinking agreeing to meet him tonight? She was only in Stone River because her father forced her to take the lead on his new subdivision project, Granite Estates. The project was being stonewalled at every turn under the leadership of another project manager. It seemed the town didn't want to be bought up and turned into an extension of Austin, but it wasn't like that mattered to Gaven Schmidt. He was a shark in the real estate business, and he always got his way. This is why he insisted Claudia pack her belongings and move to Stone River for the length of the project.

She might be a resident for the moment, but it didn't mean she was here to play with the local cowboys. In her mind's eye she could already see the disapproving look on her father's face when he heard she had even dallied with a ranch hand. He would lecture her on her breeding and class, then remind her of the money he had invested in her boarding school and etiquette lessons.

Claudia Schmidt wasn't just an average woman. No, she was a piece in her father's game of chess, a prop in his theatrical event, and a tool in his war chest, but never just a woman. Swallowing back tears of frustrated loneliness, she refused to allow herself to get depressed over things that weren't going to change. She was the only child of a wealthy and privileged only child, and that meant there was no understanding or freedom. No matter how much she would prefer to be a stay-at-home wife to a blue collar husband, and a stay-at-home mom for a pack of wild, hyperactive children.

Within moments she was parking her pretty red Benz in the tiny driveway of a two story house she had purchased to live in while she was here. It was her ideal home and the moment she had seen the listing she had called and placed an offer. It had two great perks: one, it was two miles outside the proposed borders of Granite Estates and two, it was all hers.

Two weeks after moving in, the place was just now starting to look like the home she wanted it to be. She had placed potted azaleas on the tiny front porch, and a wind chime jingled in the breeze where it hung from the eaves. The interior was still painted builders grade white as the previous family had left it, but she had selected furniture rich in color so the space was warm and inviting.

With four bedrooms and two bathrooms upstairs, she knew it was bigger than she needed, and it needed work. The kitchen cabinets were from the seventies, and the bathroom sink had a drip she had yet to fix. On the screened in back porch there were holes in the screens that needed repaired, and creaky hardwood floors ran through the whole house. It wasn't anything like the homes Schmidt Properties built. It had character and charm, and she had recently begun to consider keeping it after she finished the Granite Estates project. The hour commute would be a bitch, but it would be worth it to keep distance between herself and her father's world.

Dropping her oversized handbag on the purple sofa as she walked past, she left her shoes behind, but didn't bother to change clothes before she headed out the back door. Mack had warned her aphids would kill off the magnificent heirloom rose bush that was the showpiece of her tiny backyard if she didn't treat it quickly, and she wasn't taking any chances. Schmidt Properties and Granite Estates would have to wait fifteen more minutes.

CHAPTER THREE

"I still don't see why you had to tag along," Mack grumbled at Ryker as they walked through the gravel parking lot of Stone River's only late night entertainment. Robin's was everything a country western bar should be, dark wood, smoky air, loud music, and good beer. It had become Ryker's favorite place over the ten months he had been a resident of Stone River. He wasn't looking too closely at whether that was because it wasn't the cramped cabin he shared with Mack, or because of the alcohol.

Clapping his older brother on the shoulder, he laughed, "Because, my dear brother, I have to see this goddess among men. The way you've gone on and on about her and your *date*, you would think she was Aphrodite in the flesh."

"Just wait until you see her, Ryk. You'll be eating your arrogance. Not to mention kicking your own ass for not running to the Garden Hut for me today like I asked you to," Mack said with a shrug. It was a standard Mack Thompson reaction. Nothing ruffled the man. Which was exactly why Ryker wanted to meet the woman who had him by the nuts and all twisted up.

"So if you're already planning the wedding ceremony, tell me again why she wouldn't let you pick her up for this date?"

"She was probably playing it smart. I'm a stranger in a strange town and she's pretty small compared to me. I kinda like knowing she has enough brains to keep herself safe." Mack stopped as Ryker opened the door of Robin's. "I'm going to wait out here."

"What if she's already here?"

"She's not. Her car's not in the lot yet. Hot red Benz, can't miss it."

Ryker rolled his eyes, "Suit yourself. I'm going to get a beer."

The air in Robin's was stuffy and warm, but Ryker embraced it like a comforting blanket as he headed into the bar. Signaling the bartender for a drink, he quickly downed half of it in one large gulp. The sour taste wasn't pleasant, but the warm after burn was exactly what he needed. Half a dozen beers and he would be blissfully numb to the world again.

"Hey, Ryk! How are you, man?" Sawyer Brooks stood slightly behind and to his left holding the hand of his pretty wife, Rachel.

Forcing a semi-pleasant smile to his face, Ryker held out a hand of greeting to his friend. "I'm good. Hi, Rachel, where's the rest of your caravan tonight?"

Rachel being Rachel, didn't sense the don't-touch-me vibe he was trying to send her way, or she just chose to ignore it as she gave him a tight hug. "They are all at home. Tonight is date night for the two of us."

His face must have shown his surprise, because Sawyer snickered. "You didn't think we did everything as a quintet did you? Really? Just because I share her with my brothers doesn't mean we spent every waking moment together. We take turns sneaking away with Rachel for a few hours. Tonight is my turn."

Ryker wasn't sure how he was supposed to respond to that, so he just kept the awkward smile plastered on his face and nodded. "So you're healed up enough to dance again, huh?"

Sawyer had injured his knee late last summer thanks to a jumpy horse. He'd had surgery, and he and Ryker ended up seeing the same physical therapist and becoming fast friends.

"Yep, the only time it bothers me now is when a storm is coming through, otherwise I'm perfect," Sawyer said.

"So, what are you doing here alone?" Rachel asked, sliding onto the barstool next to him and accepting a beer from the bartender. Sawyer squeezed right in next to her, with her back pressed tightly to his chest, and his arm around her ribcage. They were like Siamese twins—and if they kept it up, he might hurl.

"Technically I'm not. Mack is meeting his date outside, and I rode in with him."

Rachel's eyes widened and her eyes narrowed, "Mack has a date? With who?"

"I don't know. Some chick he ran into at the Garden Hut. Said she has a banging body and a hot temper. She runs some sort of property business," Ryker said, waving his empty bottle at the bartender.

"Schmidt Properties is a real estate development company, and thank you for the compliment, I think." A voice rough like fine grain sandpaper on his skin filled his ears and his heart jumped. When he turned to face her, he stopped breathing. She was everything Mack said she was and more. Her blonde hair was pulled high on her head in a tight ponytail that billowed out into thick waves and hung past her shoulders. He could envision it wrapped around his fist as her full lips wrapped around his cock and her hazel eyes stared up at him full of desire.

Mack cleared his throat and Ryker could hear someone—Rachel probably—giggling softly. "This is Claudia Schmidt. Claudia, the moron who just put his foot in his mouth is my younger brother, Ryker, and these are two of my best friends, Sawyer and Rachel Brooks."

The blonde vision turned and graced their friends with welcoming easy smiles that would have brought a weaker man to his knees before she turned back to him and held out her small hand, "Nice to meet you, Ryker."

Finding his tongue was trickier than he could remember, but he managed to mutter a greeting before taking another gulp of his beer. "Do you want a beer?"

"Two please. I owe Mack a beer for his gardening assistance today."

Chuckling, Ryker met Mack's eyes and took in the warning look in their blue depths, "Are you saying all those years of helping mama in the rose beds got you a woman, bro? Damn. I knew I should have paid more attention to her."

"Schmidt Properties is buying up houses left and right. Are you planning to stay permanently, Claudia?" Rachel asked, changing the subject smoothly, and giving Ryker a chance to teach himself to breathe again.

"I'm not sure yet. I came down here for work and once I got a taste of the fresh air and sunshine I ended up buying a house to live in." Claudia accepted her beer from the bartender and passed one to Mack. "Consider us even, cowboy."

"Hardly. You'll realize how invaluable I am once you see those roses in bloom in a couple of weeks," Mack teased.

"Well, welcome to Stone River!" Rachel said with a giggle, "It's not the big city, and that's just one of its many attributes. Where did you buy your house?"

"On Lofton Road."

Rachel's eyes lit up, "Oh the two-story? With the old maple tree in the front yard?"

"Rachel is the area's top realtor," Sawyer explained proudly.

Claudia smiled, "Really? Then I'm sure we've bought property through you."

"Yes, and I thank you for it," Rachel said with a grin.

"Anyway, I fell in love with the place the moment I laid eyes on it. I've been there a couple of weeks now."

Ryker knew exactly which house she was talking about. It was white, with a dilapidated picket fence surrounding three sides of the property.

The previous owners hadn't taken the best care of it, and his respect for Claudia grew. Not many city girls would take on repairing an old country farmhouse, hell, most of the women he had dated in the past wouldn't have been caught dead in Stone River, much less purchasing a fixer upper here.

"You've got your work cut out for you on that place," Mack said, shaking his head.

"I know, but I love a challenge, and the maple tree has to be seventy or eighty years old. The branches are perfect for climbing."

Ryker snorted, "Climb trees a lot in Austin?"

"Nope, but there's always a first."

"You've never climbed a tree before?" Sawyer pressed one hand over his heart dramatically, and Rachel smacked his shoulder.

"Stop being a brat, not everyone can grow up on Brooks Pastures. Please excuse him. He and his three brothers got to live the ideal childhood on hundreds of acres of prime ranch land, so he can't comprehend some of us worked for what we have." Rachel shot Sawyer a pointed look, but he just shrugged.

When Ryker looked back to Claudia he was surprised to see her discomfited. "I had a pretty good childhood too, but climbing trees was considered extremely unladylike by my parents so it wasn't allowed. I envy anyone who had the freedom to skin their knees and get grass stains."

Looking at her with knew interest, he watched as she continued to chatter with Rachel about fixing up her new place. It seemed she was determined to do most of the work herself, and the set of her jaw told him she would try her damnedest to avoid asking for help.

Sawyer's cell phone jingled interrupting the women's conversation and he answered it with a frown. "Rogan? Yeah, sure she's right here." Passing the phone to his wife, he shrugged sheepishly at the rest of the group as Rachel directed her other husband like a drill sergeant.

"Hey, Ro, what's up? No, she's just throwing a fit. Try giving her the pink bunny that's in her crib, or try a Popsicle. Remember she's teething, so she's crankier than normal. Do you need us to come home? Okay, well, call me back if it doesn't work. Love you too, sexy."

Ryker caught the look on Claudia's face and burst out laughing. "Uh, Rach, I think you had better fill the new girl in on your four husbands before she flips out anymore."

Claudia sputtered, "Four husbands? You have *four* husbands? *Why?*"

"Yes, I have four husbands, and they are all four brothers. Rogan, Parker, Hudson, and Sawyer here." Rachel tipped her head toward Sawyer and blew him a kiss. "As for the why, well there are many reasons, but it boils down to love."

Claudia's eyes couldn't have grown wider if she stretched them with her fingers as she looked back and forth between Rachel and her husband. "How does that work exactly?"

All three of the men snickered, and Claudia looked a little embarrassed she had asked, but Rachel just shrugged. "Don't worry about it. I get that question a lot, along with many others that are much further over the line. It works because we're meant to work. As you can see we don't do everything as a group. The other three guys are home with our one year old daughter, Juliet, while Sawyer and I have a date night."

"I'm sorry, I didn't mean to be rude, but I've never heard of a woman having four husbands before. Is that legal?" Claudia looked at Mack and then Ryker, before swallowing hard. Ryker could see her body stiffen in her seat and he wondered what thoughts were going through her pretty blonde head.

"I'm only legally married to Rogan, but everyone in town knows we're polyamorous. It's unusual, but we aren't the only ones," Rachel answered, patting Claudia's hand to reassure her. "In fact, my best friend, Zoey, just married the three Keegan brothers last Christmas."

"Wow. I just...umm...wow."

Everyone laughed as Claudia tried to absorb the new information. Thankfully a local country band took the tiny bar stage and announced they would be singing the classic Gary Allen song, "Life ain't always beautiful". Immediately Sawyer and Mack took the opportunity to ask the women to dance, and the foursome left Ryker sitting alone at the bar with their drinks.

It was a metaphor for what his life had become. At one time he had been the center of every party. The star football player who was usually footing the bill for the bar tab as well as taking home his choice of the single women in attendance. One careless tackle and he was sitting on the sidelines in every possible way. His cock and his wallet regretted the move.

Sighing out his frustration, he finished off yet another beer and settled in for a long night of watching the woman of his dreams dance her sexy ass off with his older brother while asking himself why the hell he rode along. It wasn't like he needed the reminder of his new loser status.

~ ~ ~

Claudia accepted Mack's request for a dance, but she caught herself throwing glances toward Ryker every time they spun around the floor. She wasn't naïve enough to believe the smile and bravado the sad man put on.

25

There was a well of pain inside of him, and she felt a disturbing desire to wrap him in a hug and comfort him.

Even as distracted by Ryker as she was, she couldn't help but enjoy being in Mack's arms dancing. He hadn't been lying, he was a hell of a dancer, and her body fit his as though they were statues carved from the same block of clay. The fragrance of leather and man filled her nose leaving her slightly lightheaded and fully aroused. Mack and Ryker Thompson were the largest and sexiest men she had encountered since she arrived in Stone River. It was a good thing they weren't both vying for her attention because she wasn't sure she could have chosen one over the other.

Mack was barely shorter than Ryker, but they were both built like body builders. Wide at the shoulders with thick muscular thighs, that would surely have amazing stamina when necessary. Ryker was darker in coloring, and his hair was sandy brown instead of blonde. The brown hair continued down his cheeks and covered his jaw and chin in a neatly trimmed beard and mustache that looked soft to the touch. His eyes were gray blue and framed with long thick eyelashes. Between Ryker's eyes and Mack's dimples she would be a puddle of goo if she spent much time with them. She couldn't even fathom how Rachel handled being married to more than one man. Claudia couldn't seem to keep one happy for very long.

"Are you okay, sweetheart?" Mack murmured near her ear and she jumped.

"I'm fine, sorry, just a little distracted. Thank you for the dance, you've got moves, cowboy." She leaned back to look up at him from her much shorter height, raising a brow in question.

"So do you. At least a few years of dance classes under your belt if I'm not mistaken."

She snorted out a laugh, "Only about a dozen. When you're a daughter in the Schmidt family it's a given that you will have proper hobbies, such as ballet, piano, and voice lessons."

"I'll have to convince you to sing for me soon."

The subtle innuendo wasn't lost on her as his voice dropped an octave. She had no doubt in her mind he could make her whole body sing if she gave him the go ahead. Instead, she let her gaze wander around the crowded bar, refusing to acknowledge the sexual chemistry between them.

After a few moments of silence, he spoke again, "I learned to dance in my mama's living room. She insisted all men needed to know how to dance a slow song with their lady."

"Your mama sounds like an amazing woman." Claudia relaxed as he changed the subject.

"She is, well, she was."

"Oh I'm sorry. I didn't realize she had passed."

Mack shook his head and smiled, "No, she hasn't yet. She's in a nursing home in Dallas. About four years ago she was diagnosed with Alzheimer's, and she's deteriorated a lot since then. Nowadays she doesn't remember who we are when Ryker and I visit, and she has to be kept in a locked facility so she doesn't wander off for good."

Claudia could see how much it pained him, so she just nodded in agreement, "It's the best thing for her condition I suppose."

"Yeah, it is. Sometimes I wish for a few minutes with her completely clear and other times I'm glad she can't see the way things have turned out." The wistfulness in his voice grabbed at her heart and wouldn't let go.

"You seem to be doing pretty well for yourself, I'm sure she would be proud of you."

His booming laugh was followed by a tighter embrace as he slid his hands around from her hips to the curve about her ass, and tugged her closer. "You're right, she would have been proud of me even if I was living on the street. I just mean it would have been hard on her to see Ryker struggling. He's had a rough time of it lately."

Claudia glanced over at the other man, and noted the empty beer bottles stacking up in front of him, "What happened to him?"

Mack shook his head, "Not my story to tell, but suffice it to say he's in limbo right now. I suppose we both are."

"Really?" She stared up into his blue eyes as the song shifted and the band began singing a Tim McGraw hit. "What could possibly put a pair of sexy cowboys in limbo?"

~ ~ ~

Wasn't that the million dollar question? It was exactly what Mack had been asking himself for the last couple of years. Cocking his head, he winked down at her, "Sexy cowboys, huh?"

The woman was utterly gorgeous, even when she was rolling her eyes at him. She felt soft and lush against his body, and he was doing his damnedest to hold himself in check. If she felt the full power of the lust coursing through him right now, she would probably slap him back to Tuesday and take off running. Claudia continued to surprise him. Her concern for his brother, and now her concern for his own situation, made his constantly perverted thoughts even more out of place at the moment.

From the second he laid eyes on her car his body was humming, and when she climbed out wearing painted on blue jeans, boots, and a tank top held up by two tiny straps his good intentions of being a gentlemen seemed to just fizzle.

"It's a long story, better saved for our second date."

Her eyebrow rose under the sweep of her bangs and the surprise on her face nearly made him laugh. "What makes you think there will be a second date?"

"You're right. I'm jumping the gun. I haven't even kissed you yet. For all I know you might be a horrible kisser and I won't want a second date." She stared at him with wide eyes, and then suddenly she threw her head back in laughter. Loud belly rolling laughter that warmed him from the inside out.

"You are just too much, cowboy. I think I could use that beer now." She stepped away from him, and he immediately felt the loss. Refusing to allow her too much distance, he laced his fingers with hers, and let her tug him off the dance floor and back to the bar.

Ryker gave him a curious look, "What did you do? Step on her toes?"

Mack started to shake his head, but Claudia jumped to his defense.

"Nope, I'm just thirsty. Your brother is surprisingly light on his feet for someone his size." She slid her curvy backside onto the padded barstool next to Ryker, and Mack took up residence behind her, his hand resting on her hip. Something about the way Ryker smiled back at her made the hairs on the back of his neck stand on end.

He watched cautiously as she sipped her beer and chatted easily with his brother. Maybe she was distancing herself from him because he wasn't the Thompson brother she was really interested in. Suddenly his beer tasted bitter, and his stomach twisted into a knot. The two were joking with each other as though they were old friends. In fact, Mack hadn't seen Ryk look this relaxed the whole time he had been in Stone River.

"Are you hungry, Claudia? We can grab a table and order some food."

She smiled at him, and the pit in his stomach relaxed. Surely she wouldn't smile at him like that if she was really uninterested. "That would be great. I wasn't sure if they served food here or not, but I skipped lunch so I'm famished."

"As long as you're a meat eater you won't be disappointed. Robin's has the best steaks and burgers for a hundred miles," Mack answered as he looked over the heads of most everyone in the room to find a table. Sometimes being abnormally tall was a positive. "There's one over by the dart boards."

"Oh good! I can kick your ass at darts while we wait for dinner." Instead of sounding arrogant, she sounded adorably feisty, and he laughed at her challenge.

"We'll just see about that, sweetheart."

Mack's hand stayed on her waist as she rose and stepped away from the bar, keeping her beer close to protect it from a stray elbow. His throat caught when she paused before they moved two steps away, "Aren't you coming, Ryk?"

Ryker looked as surprised as Mack felt, and their eyes met over her head. It was clear on his face that his younger brother was waiting for his go ahead before interfering in his date, but Mack couldn't see a way out of it. If he didn't invite Ryk along he was going to look like a selfish ass leaving him sitting alone at the bar.

"Of course he is, he hasn't had dinner either." Mack didn't wait for Ryk's response, he just nudged Claudia along sheltering her through the crowded bar until they reached the pocket of empty space around the tiny unoccupied table. He helped Claudia up onto the tall seat and passed her one of the tiny menus he'd memorized two years ago when he moved to Stone River from Austin. "Like I said, as long as you aren't a vegetarian you can't go wrong."

She smiled as she opened the menu, "Nope, not a veggie lover, but I'm not a hunter either. I prefer not to see what my meal looked like before I eat it. Tonight a big greasy burger will be just perfect."

Ryker looked a little bit buzzed as he dropped onto one of the other empty stools. "Greasy burgers and beer? Not exactly what I would have expected for you, city girl."

Her eyebrow lifted and her lip curled, "Oh? What did you expect? Caviar and champagne? I might have grown up in the city, but I'm still a Texan."

They managed to get their food pretty quickly, and afterwards they took turns getting their asses kicked by her at darts. Ryker seemed to be knocking beers back unusually quick, and his flirtations were becoming more aggressive with Claudia. Thankfully she didn't seem to notice the subtle change, laughing and joking with the two of them equally.

Just when Mack was about to ask Claudia to dance again to get some distance from his tipsy brother, the song "Country Girl Shake if For Me" came on and the dance floor turned into lines of people all moving in the same general motion. Like a shot, Claudia was off her bar stool and dragging both Ryker and Mack to the dance floor with a laugh. "Come on, boys! If you're as country as you say you are then you should be able to line dance."

Mack fumbled to keep up with the steps as he watched her shimmy and shake in the motions of the dance. Her curvy frame swayed and jiggled in the most perfectly distracting way he could have imagined. It was clear by the look of pure primal lust on Ryker's face he was thinking the same thoughts, and the knowledge disturbed him to the core. Catching his brother's eye, Mack gave him a cold look as a warning and then watched in horror as the alcohol fuzzed version of his brother lost his mind.

CHAPTER FOUR

Claudia couldn't understand what had happened. One minute they were all dancing and having a good time, and the next minute Ryker was storming away from them through the crowded dance floor and out the front door of the bar.

By the time she and Mack reached the parking lot, he was in Mack's truck and gunning the engine so hard gravel shot up in the air. She spun away to protect her face, but really she hadn't needed to. Mack's large frame covered hers, protectively sheltering her from the storm of pebbles showering over them.

"What happened?" she asked just as Mack spun back around to glare down the road after his brother.

"Shit! He's too drunk to drive right now."

"Come on, we'll take my car and follow him. We can't stop him, but we can at least make sure we're there if he wrecks." Without pause, Claudia led the way to her car and jumped in the driver's seat. If she wasn't so concerned about Ryker, she would have laughed until she cried at the image of Mack folding his big frame into the small car. "Sorry, city girls don't drive pickup trucks."

Mack managed a wry grin before he shook his head, "No worries, I'm fine. Let's just make sure my asshole brother is too."

With him directing, she headed off into the dark countryside. It crossed her mind she should be more concerned about driving off into the dark Texas countryside with a strange man who was twice her size, but the gentle way he spoke to her and the manners he had, kept her foot on the gas. *Look at it this way, you're probably not the only woman to think serial killers don't have manners,* she thought and had to bite back a snort.

To distract herself, she started questioning Mack.

"What exactly happened in there?" His shrug didn't ease her concerns at all. "Mack, seriously, is he always this short fused?"

Dropping his head back onto the headrest, he let out a big heavy sigh. She could see the tension in his square jawline and the dimple on his cheek twitched. "He has always had a temper, but lately…Jesus."

Her only response was a raised eyebrow, but he grimaced anyway.

"A year ago, Ryker was a professional football player. In fact, he was one of the best, and he made it to the bowl game a couple of times during his ten year career after college. He had it all. Money, fame, and a future."

"What happened?"

"Damn it. He should be telling you this. It's not right I'm exposing his secrets for him." After another silent pause he sighed heavily, "He took a hit during the first game of the season late last summer, and it tore up his shoulder. At first they said he just needed surgery and physical therapy, but after the surgery the doctors told him he was done. His body couldn't take the impact of another serious hit without making his arm completely useless forever."

Claudia shook her head, "I don't understand. Lots of players get sidelined because of an injury. Couldn't he have taken a job as a coach or a broadcaster or something?"

"Oh that's not where the story ends. His accountant and business manager robbed him while he was recovering from surgery. The two disappeared with all of the money he had, leaving him high and dry. Basically he was back to square one. He had to sell off his house so he could afford to live and pay his portion of his medical bills. He moved in with me until he figures out what he wants to do with himself, but it's been almost a year and all he does is mope and drink."

Claudia glanced over at Mack to see him running his hand through his blonde curls. He looked miserable on his brother's behalf, and it tore at her heart. It wasn't fair Mack would take on Ryker's troubles and then have to deal with him pulling an immature stunt like this.

"Okay, so he's taken a few lumps, but that doesn't give him the right to act like an ass. What sent him running out of the bar?"

When Mack directed her to turn onto a gravel driveway, but ignored her question, she grunted. "Fine, don't tell me, but if it's going to be like that don't bother calling me again. I don't need this kind of drama in my life."

"Wait, Claudia—"

She shook her head, "No. I agreed to go to a bar for a beer and a dance. I did not agree to get wrapped up in your sibling's issues."

The car rolled to a stop in front of the smallest dung brown cabin she had ever seen. The porch light was on, and Mack's truck was parked in front, so clearly Ryker made his way home safely. Studiously staring ahead, she waited for Mack to get out of the car.

"Please, Claudia, give me a minute to hash this out with him and then let him apologize. I know Ryk, he's probably already feeling like shit for storming out. Please? Ten minutes and then follow me in, okay? I really like you, sweetheart, and I don't want our first date to end like this."

Her brain was telling her to put the car in reverse and get the hell out of dodge, but her heart was inside the cabin with a hurt and angry man who needed someone to knock some sense into him.

"Five minutes and if I come in and he's still acting like a toddler, I'm out. Got it?"

The smile that spread over Mack's face made her body tingle. "Got it. Damn you're sexy when you're riled up."

In a flash he was slamming out of the car and into the cabin in three leaping bounds. She barely saw the back of his head disappear through the doorway before she was left sitting in her car in the middle of nowhere alone. Dropping her head to the steering wheel, she cursed herself for giving in.

Didn't she have enough on her plate already? Her father was determined to build on the land he had purchased, but the town was putting up roadblocks and fighting him every step of the way. If she didn't manage to pull a miracle out of her ass and make it happen, her father would never forgive her. And yet, here she was getting herself hip deep in the middle of some stupid family drama between two cowboys she wasn't even sure she liked.

Immediately she chided herself for lying. She knew she liked them. Both of them. And hearing about the Brooks family had just put deliciously naughty ideas into her head about what she could do with them. She knew she was asking for trouble, but her gut told her fate dropped these two sexy Texan's into her lap for a reason. She just had to figure out if it was to help her, or hurt her.

~ ~ ~

Ryker was sitting in the easy chair with yet another beer in his hand when Mack came in. He knew he had acted like an ass, but when he saw Mack giving him the stink eye over Claudia's head it triggered an explosion of emotion in his chest. Here was a gorgeous woman, who liked beer and dancing, and wasn't afraid to stand her ground and give him some shit, and he couldn't have her because his brother got to her first. It fucking sucked.

"What in the ever-loving hell is your problem?" Mack's chest was all puffed up like he was a man on a mission and Ryker snorted.

"Nothing, I was just feeling like the third wheel and figured I better get my ass out of there before I fucked up your date. What's *your* problem?"

Mack had a temper, but it wasn't obvious. In fact, it was rare for him to get really worked up about something. Ryker was always the one who lashed out when he was upset. As a kid he was always trying to have fun, but when things didn't go his way he was easily pissed off. It was just one of the many differences in the two brothers. Their mama always compared Ryker to a hand grenade and Mack to a nuclear bomb. Both had the power to blow up and cause damage, but one was a lot more long lasting and had a greater impact with his anger. Secretly, he always envied Mack his control over his emotions, but at this moment it looked like he might have lost that prized possession.

"My problem? Really? Look you little prima donna, I know you're unhappy, but sitting here in a chair with a case of beer and a chip on your shoulder isn't going to give you any kind of future. You just risked yourself and everyone else by getting behind the wheel when you were too drunk to drive."

Ryker laughed, "I was fine! I am fine! I made it here safe and sound, so take your teat back, nanny goat, and mind your own business."

"My own business is sitting out there in her car wondering what the fuck she did wrong to send my brother on a suicide mission."

The words were like a knife to his gut. When he stormed off he never thought it might hurt Claudia. He just knew he needed to get away. "Why did you bring her here?"

"I didn't bring her. She brought me, because if you didn't notice you stole my goddamn truck and left me high and dry at Robin's."

"You could have hitched a ride."

"That's it! I'm done playing up to your melodramatic hissy fit. Grow up, Ryker! You got fucked over, you failed, you dropped the ball, whatever you want to call it. You can't go back and change it, but you sure as hell can't wipe the slate clean and start over if you won't let go of it. You are going to pull your balls out of your ass and apologize to her, or I'm going to kick your ass, little brother."

Ryker stared at his older brother in shock. Sure, Mack had given him a similar lecture six months ago, but he was nowhere near this angry then. It was as though Ryker hurting Claudia had set something off in Mack. "I didn't mean to upset her."

Mack visibly dropped as the air and tension seeped out of his lungs. "I know that, but she doesn't."

"It was just too hard to watch her, and you, and know she was untouchable."

That grabbed Mack's attention, and his jaw fell open, "What?"

"I've spent a decade dating women who couldn't hold a candle to that little firecracker, and you found her first. Not only that, but she seems genuinely interested in you, and you have nothing. No money, no house, nothing. I just don't get it."

The screen door creaked, and Ryker mimicked Mack's groan when he saw Claudia's angry visage come through the door. Cocking her blonde head to the side, she folded her arms over her chest and asked, "Are you telling me all of this was because you were jealous?"

Forcing his shame down with a gulp of his beer, Ryker gave a sharp nod. "S'pose so, sweet cheeks."

"So you actually thought it would be better to climb behind the wheel half lit and stupid, rather than just speaking up? What kind of an immature, selfish asshat are you?" Her hazel eyes were snapping fire at him, and her full lips were clenched in a tight pucker. She was beautiful to begin with but when her temper was hot, she was a sight unlike any other. His cock twitched in his pants as he skimmed his eyes over her curvy form.

Her breasts would overflow his hands, and her hips were the perfect extra curvy size to hold onto from behind. Add in the view of her plump ass and the slope of her tiny waist and she was a pin up brought to life, complete with a blonde mane of hair. He could already envision her on her knees with her soft lips parted to suck his cock and his fist wrapped in her long locks, *God she was incredible.*

"Excuse me, buddy, but my eyes are up here. If you can't remember, I have no problem blackening both of yours for you as a reminder."

He flinched at her anger, because he knew he had been caught fantasizing, but then he chuckled at her sass. Thinking about how many women he had known in his lifetime who'd salivated at the chance to have him ogle their breasts. Claudia Schmidt was probably one of the few who wasn't flattered to have his attention, but then what did he expect? He wasn't a star football player anymore, or a millionaire. He was just a down on his luck disabled has-been who barely had two nickels to his name after he paid his legal team for building a case against that lying thieving bitch of a manager and his pussy accountant. Why would this rich man's daughter, this businesswoman, want someone like him? Hell, if he tried to kiss her right now she would probably retch.

"I didn't really consider how you felt about the matter. I just knew I needed to leave. I shouldn't have forced Mack to take me along tonight. Sorry."

She was eerily quiet for several moments, her face completely devoid of emotion, but her eyes were turbulent. When she spoke her voice was

35

steady, and yet something in her stare assured him she was anything but calm.

"You're sorry. That's it. We're supposed to just go on like nothing else happened because you're sorry you broke the law, risked your life, and acted like an ass?"

"That's right, duchess. That's it in a nutshell. I fucked up, so sue me. Oh wait, you can't because I don't have shit for you to take. Can't get blood out of a turnip. Why don't you climb down off the pedestal you've put yourself on and mind your own business. I don't know why I thought you were so hot in the first place. You're just a spoiled little rich girl who thinks she's better than everyone else. Go back to Austin, duchess. You don't belong here."

The words tasted like shit as they fell off his tongue, but he couldn't stop them. Instead of sending her running, she flew at him in a rage slapping the beer bottle from his loose grip into the wall where is shattered and splashed all over the floor. Her booted foot planted in the center of the recliner's footstool right between his spread knees and she shoved it down throwing him forward. He barely managed to avoid toppling out of his seat into her.

"Do you know what? I think you're a stubborn jerk who is so deep in his own pity party he can't see the forest through the trees. You have one big thing going for you, Ryker Thompson, and he's standing right there," she gestured to Mack who was gaping at her actions in shock. "Believe it or not, I think he loves you in spite of yourself. You might have fallen on hard times, but the only reason you're a loser right now is because you are allowing it to happen. No, you are welcoming it with open arms."

Ryker stared at her in stunned fascination. *Did she really just call me a loser? Yes, I believe she did, and she's right, but it doesn't mean I want her to know it.* Jumping to his feet, he purposely stepped forward into her space to make her retreat a step. "What do you care if I'm such a loser? Disappointed the poor cowboy doesn't have a rich brother you can sweep up so you don't have to go without?"

"Ryker, that's enough damn it!" Mack's temper was barely contained. Ryker could see it on his face and in his body language. If he pushed him any harder they would end up brawling. *Hell, a good brawl might be just what I need.*

"Why? You want me to keep my mouth shut so you can get laid? She's pretty but her pussy ain't made of gold."

The words were barely out of his mouth before the pain of Claudia's fist impacting his nose set in and he fell backwards over the recliner and into the wall. The crack of his skull against the plaster never even registered in his brain before he blacked out.

~ ~ ~

"Holy shit, Claudia! You have a hell of a right hook. Ryker? Damn it to hell, he's out cold. Fuck." Mack was dragging his brother out from where he was crumpled half on and half behind the now broken easy chair.

She hadn't meant to hit him, but his arrogant attitude and insults just stung too much. When he went after Mack, she couldn't stop herself from fighting for him. Her whole hand throbbed all the way up to her elbow, and her own pain was the only thing that kept her from laughing at the fact she had just knocked out a man at least twice her size with one punch. Sure, the chair and the wall did most of the work, but damn it, she started the chain of events, and he deserved it.

"I'm sorry, Mack—" Her voice cracked as she clutched her aching arm to her belly and stared at the unconscious man in the middle of the floor.

Mack checked his brother's head to make sure he wasn't bleeding and then shook his head. "You have nothing to be sorry for. He earned every bit of the pain he'll feel later."

"Is he okay?"

"Physically? Yeah, he's fine. I don't think his head hit that hard, but he was already drunk so…"

Mack was running his hand through his yellow curls again, like he always seemed to do when he was stressed out or nervous. All of the anger had left both of them the moment she hit Ryker, and now she just felt a sad sort of pity for the unconscious man. It was clear he was in a lot of pain, but it didn't give him the right to treat her or his brother that way.

"Is your arm alright, slugger?"

The question caught her off guard and she looked up at him in surprise. His concerned blue eyes were taking in the way she held her injured hand against her body protectively. "Uh, I think so. I don't know."

"We better get some ice on it and check to see if you broke anything, sweetheart. Come on." His large body was invading her space again, but she didn't feel awkward about it this time. In fact, she felt safe and secure as he wrapped one arm around her shoulders and propelled her toward the kitchen.

"Are you sure he's okay? Maybe we shouldn't leave him?"

"He'll be fine once he sleeps off his drunken stupidity," he answered as he retrieved an ice pack from the freezer and moved back to her side.

She gasped in surprise when his hands landed on her hips and he lifted her easily up onto the kitchen counter in front of him so she was easier to reach. "Mack!"

"Yes, sweetheart?"

A hiss of pain slipped from between her teeth when he began checking each knuckle and finger gently, and she couldn't think straight. Between the pain in her hand and the heat of his callused finger tips, she felt completely out of control as sensations barreled through her.

"I don't think anything is broken, but you won't be shaking anyone's hand for the next week or so. Pretty impressive for a city girl."

The glint of humor in his gaze eased some of her discomfort and she gave him a small smile. "Even in the city we stick up for our friends."

"Is that what we are, Claudia? Friends?"

She felt her lips part as she stared up at him. Did he know what his tone did to her? The slight curl of his upper lip told her he did, and turned her on even more. She wanted to taste him, now more than ever before.

"I hope so. I-I mean, I did just coldcock your brother and knock him out, but if you don't hold that against me—"

His laughter cracked through the air, "Hold it against you? Hell, honey, it's more likely to make me fall in love with you. Ryker has needed someone to knock some sense into him for a while. I just kept thinking he needed more time and space to get over it. I kept telling myself everyone deals with their issues differently. I ran off to The Cage when my business went under, but Ryker doesn't have an outlet. All of his so-called friends are back in Chicago avoiding his calls."

"What's The Cage?" The question seemed to rattle him, and he stopped speaking and grimaced.

"Uh, it's just a local club."

Curiosity got the better of her, and she prodded the subject even though he clearly didn't want to talk about it. "Like a dance club?"

"No, uh, shit. Look this is our first date, and it hasn't exactly been run of the mill, but I'm still hoping I haven't scared you off completely yet."

She almost laughed at the awkward look on his face. Didn't he notice she was sitting on the counter in his kitchen, with ice pressed to her bruised hand, and his lean hips between her spread knees? This was clearly not a typical situation, and if she hadn't gone running when his brother took off driving drunk, or when he insulted her in every possible way...but the more she watched him fidget, the more her curiosity ate at her. Something about the club had triggered his awkwardness. What kind of club would make someone that uncomfortable?

"Is it a strip club? Or a gentleman's club? Like an escort service? Is that it? You paid for sex with a prostitute and now you're feeling guilty?"

Wide blue eyes stared at her for a few brief seconds before he was laughing again. When his laughter finally calmed, he gripped her jaw gently and ran his thumb over her bottom lip. Her tongue darted out to wet it and his pupils dilated. "No, you nosey woman, I have never paid for sex in my life. The Cage is a BDSM club where I'm a member."

Nothing prepared her for that. Her mouth fell open as he smirked at her shock. "BDSM? You like to beat on women?"

He shook his head and rolled his eyes, "No, sweetheart. That's not what BDSM is about. Sometime in the near future we will continue this conversation and I will try to explain, but I think after all of this excitement now is not the time."

She wanted desperately to question him further. To understand what he meant by BDSM club. It's not like she was a complete moron. She had read the popular books, so she knew the basics. People into that stuff liked to inflict pain on others and make them beg and cry. The sour taste in her mouth and the butterflies in her belly had her nodding her agreement to shelve the topic for another time. Too much had happened tonight for her to absorb the man she thought she was interested in, was way too kinky for her plain-Jane self.

"Are you sure Ryker is okay?"

"Let's go check, before I walk you to your car."

Mack helped her off the counter and they both went back into the living room. The big man on the floor had shifted and thrown one arm over his face and he was snoring. Reassured he really was just sleeping off the alcohol, she picked up her keys from where she had dropped them earlier and led the way out of the tiny cabin to her car.

She paused before opening the car door and turned to face Mack. In the dark shadows of night he seemed more raw and dangerous, and her heart fluttered a little in her chest.

"I wish—"

"I'm sorry—"

They both started to speak at the same time, and broke off with a laugh. Mack shook his head, "If you're going to try to apologize again, you may as well keep quiet. This wasn't your fault in any way. It's been coming for a long time."

She nodded and stared at the button in the center of his wide chest in silence. His hands came up to wrap around each of her elbows and he rubbed up and down as though trying to warm her. If he only knew how hot she already was for him.

"I was going to say I wish this night had gone differently, Claudia. I will make it up to you on our second date." His warm breath caressed her cheek as he dipped his head down, and instinctively she lifted her face.

"There you go again, assuming there will be a second date." She drew back, but her voice was so breathless he just grinned. Even in the dim moonlight she could see the deep groove of his dimples and the white flash of his teeth. The man had a killer smile to go with his sex God body.

"There will be."

Three words, and her knees nearly collapsed. The confidence and command in those three words sent goosebumps skittering across her skin and she struggled to maintain her dignity. What would he think if she begged him to touch her right now?

"Sweetheart, I'm going to give you five seconds to get in your car and shut the door, because if you don't I'm going to kiss you, and once I kiss you, I have a feeling there will be no going back for us."

She let out a gasp of indignation and then her breath caught. He was serious. Torn between the desperate desire to finally taste him and her own instinct for self-preservation, she swayed on her feet. Only his hands on her biceps kept her from toppling.

"Five...four..."

She jerked backwards and both of her hands landed on the center of his chest. Just the physical connection made her pussy throb and her skin burn.

"Three...two..."

Her mind was spinning as she pressed one hand to his chest, "Wait a second. Don't I get a say in this? Who says I even want you to kiss me?"

"You're still standing here."

Lightning struck the moment their lips touched. Fire sizzled through her veins, and pooled directly between her thighs. She gasped on impact and he took it as an invitation to invade her mouth. That's exactly what it was, an invasion. Her senses were completely overwhelmed and she melted into him, her arms sliding up around his neck as he braced himself on the car behind her with one hand and tugged her body tightly to him with the other.

Somewhere in the recesses of her brain she heard a tiny voice warning her about getting involved when there were so many hurdles between them, but in that moment she couldn't hold on to it. There was no gap too wide or mountain too high when his mouth and hands were on her body. Instead, she felt as though she had finally found a home. A safe place where she could revel in this one man's desire and need for her.

It could have been hours, but she knew it was only minutes before they broke apart panting for air, and she buried her face in the crook of his neck. Only the chirping of crickets sounded on the breeze as the two of them fought to regain control over themselves.

"I'm—"

He jerked back a step, and covered her mouth with his hand. "Don't you dare say, you're sorry. Baby, if I could, I'd strip you naked right here and fuck you seven ways to Sunday, but you deserve better. We didn't have the best first date, but that kiss assures me that it wasn't the worst either. Give me your phone."

She shook her head trying to follow his train of thought, "My phone?"

"Yes, love. I want to put my number in it, so you can call me when you get home."

Somehow she managed to open the car door and fish her cell phone out of her purse, handing it to him silently. She watched while his thick thumbs zipped over the tiny device like a pro, and a buzzing sounded from his back pocket. He pulled his own phone out and smiled again, "There, all set. Call me as soon as you're there, okay?"

Her tongue wouldn't work. Something in his kiss must have numbed her mouth. Like some sort of anesthetic because her voice box seemed frozen too.

"Claudia, okay?"

Resorting to a silent nod, she accepted her phone back and took a seat in the car.

"Take a left when you get to the road, and then a right when you see the sign for Dottie's Ice Cream Parlor. That will get you back to Main Street."

She nodded again and shut the car door, latching her seatbelt as quickly as possible. His large frame filled her view as she backed up and turned around. He remained standing in place until she turned out of the drive toward town and he disappeared in the darkness.

Within fifteen minutes she was pulling into her own driveway, still in shock over the whole evening. It was sure as hell the strangest first date she had ever been on. As she entered her house and began stripping her clothes for a shower, she pulled out her phone again and sent Mack a quick text. *I'm home, safe and sound.*

A couple seconds later her phone chirped with a response. *I thought I told you to call me.*

She rolled her eyes as she answered. *Does it make a difference?*

Turning on the shower, she read his response. *We'll work on following instructions.*

She giggled as she sent the next message. *What are you going to do? Spank me?*

His next response took longer, and she began to question her teasing while she waited. What if he didn't get the joke? Her heart jumped when she read the next message. *Anytime. Anyplace. I'll see you in my dreams. Goodnight.*

Just like that he flipped the script again leaving her weak-kneed and confused. His offer to spank her shouldn't make her stomach clench and her pussy weep, right? Choosing the safest road, she sent him a quick, *Goodnight*, and climbed into the shower, already wondering about date number two.

CHAPTER FIVE

Twelve hours and two pots of coffee later, Ryker felt like a complete chump. He couldn't believe he had acted the way he did, especially with Claudia. She didn't deserve it. In fact, she was completely right about his lashing out because he was hurting. The irony that the spitfire managed to bring him down with one sharp punch to the nose wasn't lost on him, but he didn't feel the need to examine it too closely.

He hadn't seen Mack yet today. When he woke up on the floor of the cabin, he was alone. The smell of alcohol was as strong on his breath as the bitter aftertaste was on his tongue, and his head felt like someone had been using Mack's leatherworking mallet on it. After a shower, he managed to force down some aspirin with his coffee while he debated what his next move was.

Claudia's reaction to his rudeness made him wonder if perhaps her attraction to him was stronger than she was letting on. True, they barely knew each other, but already he felt like she was some sort of puzzle piece that had been missing from his world. Now that he found her he wasn't sure he wanted to let her out of his sight, at least not until he knew how she fit into his life. He wasn't a complete idiot, even if his actions from the night before proved otherwise. He was fully aware Mack wanted to keep her for himself, but Ryker wasn't about to step aside just yet.

She seemed intrigued by the idea of a ménage, but no amount of self-reflection made him want to test those waters. As much as he loved his brother, he really had no desire to see him naked and screwing his woman. He just couldn't figure out how to let her know he shared her feelings without looking like a bigger asshole than he already did. Stealing Mack's woman might just rip apart the tenuous strings holding the brothers together, but Ryker couldn't let Claudia go without giving it a shot, and the only chance he had of getting back in her good graces was to man up and apologize.

Leaving a note on the counter for Mack that just read, "Be back later," he headed into town in search of her. It was a Saturday, so he was hoping she would be at home, but when he pulled into her driveway his heart skipped a beat.

Perched atop an eight foot ladder was the woman of his dreams. Her footing was precarious, and she had one hand braced on a window ledge while she held a paint scraper in the other and she was viciously attacking the peeling paint off the clapboard siding in front of her. To his eyes it looked like if the wind blew wrong she was going to topple, and he didn't hesitate to leap out of his car running full steam in her direction.

"Ryker?" she asked, frowning down at him as he reached the bottom of her wobbly ladder and secured it firmly in his grip. "What are you doing here?"

"The better question is what are you doing up there, duchess? You're going to break your neck!"

Yesterday he believed it was impossible for him to ever feel protective of a woman again. It had been a woman who had taken his trust and torn it to shreds just last summer, but at the moment he couldn't seem to stop thinking about all of the horrific outcomes a fall would bring to this petite beauty.

"I'm scraping paint. What does it look like? Why do you care?" she snapped back, managing to cock her hip and look indignant without wobbling on the narrow ladder step.

"Sweet cheeks, I know what you're doing, but I don't understand why? This ladder isn't nearly tall enough for this project, and neither are you. Not to mention you could have just asked for a hand. Me and Mack—"

"You and Mack? So you're speaking now? After last night's show I wouldn't have blamed him if he never spoke to you again. And why would I bother to ask you for help, Ryker? You made it pretty clear what you thought of me right before I punched you in your face, remember?" Her hair was pulled back in a messy bun, and her gorgeous face was pinched in a tight frown as she glared down at him.

Risking her wrath, he wrapped his hand around her ankle, and squeezed. "Please, Claudia. I came here to apologize. I'd rather do it face to face. Will you come down?"

For a moment he thought she was going to refuse. Her body remained tense and she twirled the paint scraper in her hand while she thought over his request. When she finally jammed the handle of the tool in the back pocket of her shorts, he sighed with relief.

"I'll come down, but only because I want to be able to look you in the eye when I tell you to fuck off."

He didn't move back as she began to make her way down the ladder, so she ended up in the circle of his arms. She smelled sweet, and now that he was closer he could see the streaks of dirt and sweat on her face, and the tiny curls of hair escaping her bun to dance on the nape of her neck. It was damn tempting to place a kiss there, but the hostility oozing off her told him it wouldn't be appreciated right now.

"Back up, Thompson. You're too close." Her voice was wobbly and breathy, but her tone was determined and he took a step back, letting his arms fall to his sides. She spun around and crossed her arms under her lush breasts, lifting them in the tank top she wore so he got a fantastic view of her cleavage. He had to swallow hard and shake himself when she spoke again, "Well, get on with it. As you can see I have work to do, so I can't stand around chatting."

Her hazel eyes were narrowed on his face, but he couldn't meet her gaze. It was harder than he imagined, but he was determined to apologize. "Claudia, I'm sorry. I screwed up last night."

When he didn't say anything else for a couple of moments, she huffed, "You're damn right you did. You could have killed someone."

Eyes wide he laughed, "I didn't mean—well I did, but that's not exactly what I was apologizing for. I meant about what I said to you and Mack last night. I was angry and I lashed out at you. You didn't deserve it, and I didn't mean it. I'm sorry."

"So you're sorry for hurting my feelings, but not for driving drunk?" she asked, sounding even angrier, "Why doesn't that surprise me?"

Shock rocked him on his heels when she spun away from him and marched up her front steps into her front door. Anger warred with confusion in his head, and he followed her flaring temper. The screen door creaked as he went through it and somewhere in his distracted brain he made a note to bring a can of WD40 with him when he visited next time.

Her living room was decorated in bright colors and patterns that made him slightly dizzy, so he followed the sounds of life down the hallway into a small kitchen that had seen better days. The best feature was the top of the line appliances that were obviously just off the showroom floor.

Zeroing in on his target, he froze in his tracks as she lifted a glass of ice water to her lips and took a big swallow. His gaze followed the column of her throat as it bobbed, and suddenly his jeans were way too tight. Widening his stance, he crossed his arms and glared at her with as much intensity as he could muster with a hard-on. "You know when a man apologizes to you, you should at least be courteous enough to accept it civilly."

"I don't accept it. Civilly or otherwise," she said, dabbing her lips and then her sweaty forehead and neck with a hand towel. "That shade of purple looks lovely on you by the way."

Confused, he looked down at his clothes before realizing she was talking about the bruise on his face. "Are you always this difficult?"

One side of her lips curved up, "Pretty much. Are you?"

Fighting back a grin, he nodded, "Yep. Look, I am sorry about getting behind the wheel. I don't normally do that kind of thing. It was reckless and irresponsible, and then I followed it up by being immature and hateful." He paused and waited for a reaction, but her face remained completely emotionless. "I would really like the chance to start over, and forget last night ever happened. Please?"

The only sound in the house was the drip of water as he waited for her response. He added the leaking kitchen faucet to his mental list of fixes but kept his eyes firmly trained on her face.

"I'll agree to a truce and accept your apology, but I promise you, Ryker Thompson, if you pull a stunt like that again, I'll call the cops after I beat the snot out of you myself." Her tone was so serious he nodded solemnly.

Claudia spun around and refilled her empty glass of water, taking another big drink before she spoke again, "Where's Mack?"

"I don't know. He was gone when I got up."

Her eyes widened and she stared back at him in shock. "You came to me before you talked to him? Why?"

This was his chance to lay it all out there. Moving closer to her, he took her glass from her hand and set it on the counter before cupping her jaw. "When I woke up all I could think about was getting to you and convincing you to forgive me, duchess. It never crossed my mind to look for him first."

Her dainty pink tongue flicked out to lick her lips and he saw her anxiety rise as he boxed her in against the counter. "I don't understand, Ryk. Mack's your brother, you should—"

"Mack's a big boy. We've had much worse fights, trust me. I'll talk to him later and we'll clear the air. You were my first priority." He let his thumb stroke the line of her jaw before caressing her bottom lip. It was plump and so soft to the touch he almost groaned out loud. Lifting his other hand, he took her hair in his hand forcing her to tip her head back. If he had any doubts about her desire for him, they were gone in an instant because her pupils dilated and her mouth dropped open on a gasp.

"Ryker, we can't."

"Why not, Claudia? Who's stopping us?" he murmured, tightening his grip on her hair and her jaw.

"Mack." The one word came out in a breathless whisper.

Smiling, Ryker lowered his mouth until they were close enough to share a breath. "He isn't here, duchess. I am. And you want me as much as I want you."

He gave her another moment to say no, and then he lowered his mouth capturing her lips in a scorching hot kiss. It burned through his body, searing his soul and branding his heart with her essence. Everything ceased to matter in that moment as he plundered her with a kiss and she took possession of him.

After a pause, her tongue sought his, and she stroked his lips inviting him into her warmth. Somewhere in the back of his brain he registered when her hands slid up his chest and around his neck to hold him in place. It gave him the opening to drop both hands to her hips and lift her so she was seated on the kitchen counter, making their kiss more comfortable, and bringing his hips into alignment with the V of her thighs. His groin rocked in an instinctive motion, as her ankles crossed behind him, pulling him closer.

The sounds she made in her throat were making his balls tighten, and he fought for control of himself as he made love to her mouth. When she finally tore her lips away from his, and stared up into his eyes still gasping, he could see guilt and desire at war in their golden depths. Neither one of them spoke, but her ankles released him, so he took an awkward step back to give her more room. His cock was throbbing behind his zipper, and his bruised face ached where they had been pressed so tightly together, but he felt like a God when she looked at him with lust in her eyes.

"I can't do this with you. I'm seeing Mack, and it wouldn't be fair to him. I'm not the type of person to cheat on a man."

"I'm sorry, I didn't realize you two were exclusive already."

She shook her head groaning in frustration, "We're not, but considering I was kissing him last night, it doesn't seem like he would be thrilled I'm making out with you this morning."

"I want you, Claudia. I know you met my brother first, but I had to make it known I'm in this to win you for myself." He pressed a kiss her palm before helping her off the counter, steadying her when she swayed.

"I'm not a prize at a carnival, Ryk," she responded, staring at the center of his chest.

"No, you're worth so much more, duchess."

In an instant the desire and anxiety on her face was replaced with fury, and she gave him a hard shove knocking him backwards into the opposite counter. "So that's what this is about? You're broke now, and Mack found a rich girl, so you want to steal me and my fortune away? Miss the good life, huh, Ryker?"

His own temper reacted and he grabbed her wrists, keeping her from storming away or throwing another punch, "No, Claudia. I don't give a damn about your money. I want you. I want the Texas girl that drinks beer, talks back, and dances till her feet ache. The girl who plays darts better than any man I know, and takes stupid chances like standing on a ladder as old as my grandma to scrape a house that's seen more generations than a cat has lives. Fuck. Do all of the men you know have ulterior motives?"

Pain filled her wide eyes, and a flush of pink stole up her cheeks. She looked torn between anger and shock, so he took a chance and pulled her into his arms, hugging her tightly against his chest.

"Believe me, Claudia, please. I think we could have something good between us if we'd both just lower our damn defenses. All I'm asking is for a chance. Let me take you out, or we'll stay in. Hell, I'll help you weed your roses, just give me a chance to make amends for last night's stupidity and show you who I really am. Surely, my brother wouldn't complain about me hanging out with you helping you fix up your house as friends."

After a few tense breaths she nodded, and whispered, "Okay, but only as friends. And if we're staying in you're going to have to bring your own paint scraper. I only have one."

He laughed as the anxiety eased in his chest, and he breathed easier. "Deal. In fact I'll run in town to The Garden Hut now and pick one up. I'll grab us some lunch too if you haven't eaten."

She shook her head, "Can you eat with a hangover?"

Winking at her, he gave her his brightest smile, "For you I can do anything, sweet cheeks. Do you need anything else while I'm in town?"

"Uh, I was going to go in later and get some paint stripper. I took the old shutters down to repaint them and realized they had like umpteen layers of paint on them already."

"Done. I'll be back before you know it." He turned and started for the front door, but stopped short to look back over his shoulder at her, "And, Claudia, do me a favor and stay off the ladder. You nearly gave me a heart attack earlier. I'll get the upper stuff when I get back."

When she laughed and nodded her agreement, he hurried out to his car feeling better about his life than he had for nearly a year.

~ ~ ~

Claudia's heart continued to thud in her chest like a stampede of horses for several long minutes after Ryker's car left her driveway. Her panties clung to her pussy lips, damp with the moisture of her desire for him, and her scalp still tingled from the tugs on her hair.

No matter which way she spun it she knew she was in trouble. Mack intended for them to be seeing one another faithfully, and she knew it would hurt him more because it was his brother.

Ryker might say the words she wanted to hear, but he didn't mean them. He wasn't going to accept a friendship when the spark between them was so hot. That was obvious after just one kiss. The biggest problem was she wanted him just as much as she wanted Mack. They were very different from each other, and yet she felt the same connection with both of them. Something deep inside of her was happier when she was in the presence of the Thompson brothers, and it unnerved her a bit.

Her thoughts were interrupted by the tinkling sound of her cell phone, and she cursed as she ran to look for it. She had a bad habit of laying it down wherever she was when she hung up and then forgetting where it was. It jingled away for several seconds before chiming a new voicemail was available as though punctuating the fact she had missed the call. When she finally located it on the bathroom countertop where she left it last night before taking her shower, she regretted listening to the message the moment she heard her father's voice.

"Claudia, this is your father." Like she didn't already know who it was. She rolled her eyes as he continued, "I'm following up on the Granite Estates project. We got a fax today that the Stone River planning board is holding a town hall meeting this week. You need to be there, Claudia. This project must proceed without hindrance." He cleared his throat, "Uh, I hope you're well. Call your mother soon so she doesn't worry."

The message clicked off, and she attempted to slide the phone into her back pocket, knocking the paint scraper to the floor with a clatter. She jumped nearly a foot when the doorbell rang a minute later.

Seriously, this place is like Grand Central Station all of a sudden.

Pondering how Ryker had managed to get to the store and back so quickly, she was frowning as she tugged open the heavy door. To her surprise, Mack was standing outside her front door, holding a bouquet of daisies that were clearly just picked. Her heart flip-flopped when his face lit up in a brilliant smile. He reminded her of a kid with his clear blue eyes, blonde curls, and dimples.

"Hi, sweetheart."

"Mack! What are you doing here?" She held the door open as wide as possible, but with his broad shoulders he still had to turn to fit through the opening beside her.

Handing her the bouquet, he wrapped an arm around her waist. "I was thinking about you and wanted to come see you in the light of day. Is that okay? I'm not interrupting anything, am I?"

"Uh, no it's fine. I'm just scraping paint off the house today. Let me go put these in water." She started to twist out of his grip, but he stopped her with one hand on her jaw.

His eyes narrowed, "You seem tense. Does it upset you that I came over, Claudia?"

Stilling in his hands, she sighed, "No. Actually I'm glad you did. I wanted to see you again after last night."

Pure male satisfaction lifted the corners of his lips into a smirk, and he dipped his head to claim a kiss from her, stopping her words. His kiss was so different from his younger brother's it made her gut twist with guilt. As much as she enjoyed it, she couldn't continue without telling him the truth. Forcing one hand up to his chest, she pushed a little, breaking their kiss.

"Mack, stop. We need to talk."

His hands dropped away from her and he cursed. "I'm moving too fast for you, right? I'm sorry for pushing you, sweetheart, I'll ease up."

"Damn it, would you let me explain before you get all worked up," she snapped. "What is it about you two Thompson brothers that impedes the connection between your ears and your tongue? I want to kiss you, Mack, I happen to enjoy it. A lot. But you need to know Ryker showed up here just a little while ago."

"What did he say? Did he upset you?" His instant anger on her behalf was sweet considering he thought she and Ryker were still at odds.

"No, he apologized profusely, and then he kissed me."

Mack's mouth fell open and he stared at her in shock. There wasn't any other emotion on his face. No anger, or betrayal, just pure confused shock. "He what?"

"He kissed me, and I kissed him back—" Mack took a step backwards away from her, and she hurried to put the daisies down on the sofa table so she could reach for him. Gripping his hand with hers, she held him in place while she continued, "I stopped it, Mack. I told him you and I met first and until we agreed otherwise I was off limits."

His head cocked to the side, and a small smile lifted his lips again, "You did?"

Nodding, she continued, "I did. I'm not the type of woman to play you two against each other, and I needed you to hear it from me. I like you a lot, Mack, and while I'm in Stone River I would like to keep seeing you, but not at the expense of your relationship with your brother."

"Well I'll be jiggered. Ryker's a smooth one, that's for sure. I never dreamed he would attempt to go for you after last night's knock out round. What did he say when you told him you weren't interested?" Mack asked, his fingers laced through hers, and she sighed with relief he wasn't angry.

"I didn't say I wasn't interested. I told him I couldn't hurt you by going behind your back. Anyway, he said he is in it to win it, or some other such nonsense. He agreed to a friendship when I told him that was all I could offer. He's actually coming back here shortly to help me with the paint scraping today."

Mack snorted out a laugh, "Oh I'm sure he's playing for the win. Ryker is competitive by nature, and he sees this as another game."

Claudia considered that angle, and the longer she thought about it the madder she got. If Ryker really did see winning her heart as just another way to one up his brother, then she wasn't going to make it easy for him. It also burned her ass a little that Mack didn't take the competition seriously. It was almost like he didn't think Ryker really was interested in her.

"There will be no competition because I'm not playing games, with either one of you." She released Mack's hand and scooped the daisies up, "I'm going to put these in water. You're welcome to stay and help, but I only have one paint scraper."

The sound of a car door punctuated her statement, and she hurried to disappear in the kitchen like a coward. Mack and Ryker could hash out their differences without her around. Unable to locate any sort of vase, she settled on a mason jar for her flowers and took her time arranging them before she set them in the center of her dining table. They were the kind of tiny white daisies you might see on the side of the road while you were driving. Beautiful, but unlikely to survive very long, and a moment of melancholy swept through her as she realized they likely represented the relationship she would have with Mack. It wasn't like he was going to pack and move to Austin with her when she finished the Granite Estates project. The subdivision would likely take several years to complete, though, so it was possible they wouldn't even be into each other by then.

Forcing her feet to carry her back into the living room, she found Mack and Ryker quietly conversing just in front of the door. They both looked up when they spotted her, and smiled.

"Okay, that's a good sign. No blood on my floors, no new bruises..." she looked pointedly at the bruise she had left on the Ryker's face the night before, "and you're smiling. Does this mean we're all friends?"

"I already told you we were friends, duchess. Mack and I were just discussing—"

"Who was going to scrape paint and who was going to fix your squeaky screen door," Mack interrupted, and Ryker frowned slightly. She wasn't a moron, she knew they hadn't been discussing the house chores, but she wasn't ready to touch the alternative topic of conversation so she went with it.

"You guys don't have to help you know?"

They both seemed to roll their eyes in unison, before Mack spoke, "I'll be glad to help, but tell me, why are you putting so much work into this house if you're planning on moving back to Austin?"

He followed her out the front door, as she answered, "I love to work with my hands on projects. I always have. My father doesn't think there's a life in being an artist or I might have pursued it. This is the first chance I've had to buy an old place and really fix it up. If I'm going to be here for a couple of years working on the subdivision project, then I wanted to have a home I could enjoy."

"I hate to ask this, sweetheart, but what if the project doesn't happen? Last I heard the planning board and the council weren't thrilled about the idea." Mack's words made her hands sweaty. That was exactly the problem. She needed this project to prove to her dad she could follow in his footsteps and take over the business someday. His approval was too important for this to fail.

"I'm a Schmidt. We don't deal in what ifs, we make things happen. There is a town hall meeting this week, and I intend on convincing them all that this project will bring new residents to the community and with them new funds for roads, schools, and growth."

Ryker stood on the front steps casually leaning against the railing, grinning. "Good luck with that. This is small town Texas. They don't have much interest in growth."

"Then I will make them interested in it. Granite Estates is the best thing that could happen to Stone River," she said, with an arrogant toss of her head.

Mack cleared his throat, "I beg to differ." He reached out and grabbed her hand, tugging her into his chest for a kiss. When he released her lips, she was wide-eyed and breathing hard. "You're the best thing to ever happen to Stone River, sweetheart."

Her eyes darted over to Ryker who was frowning at their embrace, and she felt guilt rush through her. She didn't want to hurt his feelings or make things awkward. He shifted in place and grumbled, "Before you two start humping in the grass, Claudia needs to eat her sandwich." For the first time she noticed the white paper bag in his hand. He shook it at her, and asked, "Do you need a plate to eat off, or can you tolerate a napkin just this once, duchess?"

She groaned, "You know, just when I start to think you might be a halfway decent guy you open your mouth."

He feigned shock, "And here I brought you only the finest of club sandwiches our local diner can create."

Mack laughed at their back and forth banter, and took the paint scraper from her hand, "You go eat, baby. I'll get started on the scraping, and when Ryker finishes his fine dining experience he can work on the screen door."

Claudia and Ryker settled on the porch steps to eat their sandwiches. From the first bite she was hooked. Turning her surprise on Ryker, she commented, "This really is an amazing sandwich."

"I told you. Want to know what the secret ingredient is?" He looked around before leaning in conspiratorially, and when she nodded he whispered, "French dressing. On the third piece of bread in the middle they spread some French salad dressing in there, and it gives it a little extra something."

Her laughter bounced off the house behind them, and echoed out into the yard startling a bird perched in the maple tree. "Who would have thought? Thank you for the sandwich, Ryk. It's delicious."

"You're welcome, duchess. I can be a nice guy sometimes, just don't get used to it." He winked at her, and shoved their trash back into the paper bag before standing. "We better get back to work. I heard the boss on this job is a real tough bitch." He went back into the house to dispose of the trash, leaving her laughing behind him as she retrieved the second paint scraper.

For a few moments she just observed Mack as he worked, admiring the ripple of muscles under his t-shirt, and the clenching of his tight ass every time he reached his arm out. He had a body built for sin, and she considered coercing him down off the ladder just to get her hands on him again. The thought vanished the instant it appeared, because if Ryker walked out and found them in any kind of erotic embrace she knew it would wound him deeply, and she didn't want to do that. Hurting either of them was the last thing she wanted to do.

When he turned and met her gaze, he frowned, "Everything okay, sweetheart?"

"Are you sure you're okay with Ryker being here?" she asked hesitantly. She needed to know, but she wasn't sure she would be able to send Ryk away if Mack wanted her to.

He lowered his arm, and slowly climbed down the ladder until he stood face to face with her. Giving her a small smile, he sighed, "No. Not necessarily, but I love my brother, and as much as I want to be alone with you, I don't want to hurt him. I'm not sure what the future holds for you and me, but I hate to think something this good would cause my brother pain."

She nodded in understanding. "I don't want to be caught in the middle."

"You won't be. I won't let it happen. Give Ryk some time to get it through his head you and I are together, and he'll ease off. I do want you two to be friends, even though I want you all to myself." He bent and kissed her forehead. "Stop worrying, or you'll make yourself sick. Ryk and I have been competing for things our whole lives. He just has to realize I already won the prize."

Mack climbed back up the ladder and set to work again, leaving her alone with her thoughts and the cracked paint in front of her to take out her stress on. She wondered if she should explain to Mack that she was really attracted to Ryker, but the thought filled her with dread. It was important not to shake his confidence, because as far as she was concerned, she was Mack's girl for the moment. She met him first, and so far he had been nothing but wonderful to her. Besides, she was only here temporarily. She needed to make sure these two brothers still had a good relationship when she left.

With Mack working on the ladder and her on the lower half, they were making good progress and an hour had passed before Ryker's voice behind her made her jump. "Screen doors are both oiled, so they don't squeak now, and I fixed the leak in your kitchen faucet. While I was there I fixed the garbage disposal too."

"You did all of that already?" she asked in shock.

He shrugged, "Yeah, it wasn't a big deal. All easy fixes."

"Well I'm impressed."

His eyes narrowed, "Why?"

"Because I wouldn't have expected a big shot football star to be able to fix a garbage disposal," she teased, laughing when he let out a loud huff.

"I might have played pro football for ten years, but I lived with my daddy for eighteen, and he didn't believe in hiring a repairman. Mack and I have all sorts of random knowledge in our heads thanks to him," Ryker said, holding his hand out to her. She just looked at it curiously. "The scraper. Your hands are already raw, if you keep it up they will look like ground meat. I'll take over."

A quick glance down at her knuckles revealed the truth of his words, and she wrinkled her nose. "I can finish. We're almost done. I just wanted to get this side done today, and then tomorrow I can put primer on it. I'll leave it that way until I'm ready to paint the whole thing."

Out of the corner of her eye she saw Mack shift to watch from atop the ladder, and both he and Ryker were frowning at her. Ryker's voice was smooth, but firm, "Claudia, I never thought for a second you *couldn't* do it. I just don't want you to when I'm available to help you."

"But—"

"Stop arguing, sweetheart. It won't do you any good. Neither one of us is going to sit back on our heels and watch you work your fingers to the bone," Mack said from above her, and she grunted a non-response before holding the scraper out to Ryker.

"Ganging up on me already, huh? That won't always work for you, but I'll give in this time. I'll go get us something to drink while you two finish. We can all go sit in the shade on the back porch when it's done."

"Sounds like heaven, sweetheart."

Ryker nodded his agreement, "We'll meet you back there, sweet cheeks."

Irritated by his choice of endearments she rolled her eyes at him and went inside. Within twenty minutes she had a pitcher of lemonade and a plate of Oreos ready as the guys came through the front door.

"Oreos?" Mack said with a smile.

Ryker's mouth dropped open and he rubbed at his chest over his heart, "You're a goddess! How did you know my favorite cookies were Oreos?"

She laughed, "I didn't, but they are *my* favorite and currently the only cookie in the house."

He suddenly looked serious, "Do you have more?"

Nodding, she frowned, "Yeah, another package in the cupboard. Why?"

Scooping up the plate she had so neatly arranged, he darted toward the back door without a word. Claudia gaped after him in shock and Mack laughed.

"If you want any, you had better get out the other package, sweetheart. Oreos are a weakness of his. You won't even get a crumb off the plate without sacrificing your first born," Mack explained.

Narrowing her eyes, she marched after Ryker, "We'll just see about that."

Sure enough, he was noshing on the cookies as he lounged in a lawn chair on the back porch. His long legs were stretched out in front of him so his ass was perched on the edge of the chair. The hem of his t-shirt rose slightly, exposing a slim line of tan skin and the brown curls of hair that led from somewhere under his shirt, to his jeans and beyond. She almost reached out to feel how soft or springy those curly hairs were, but caught herself just in time.

For God's sake, Claudia, you just finished telling him you were off limits and now you want to molest the man on your porch.

She shook her head and crossed her arms as she stood in front of him. "Ryker, you're sharing those cookies."

"No I'm not," he mumbled through a mouthful of crumbs. "Consider it payment for the job well done."

"I'll write you a check instead. Give 'em."

She held out her hand and for a moment she thought he might give her the plate. At the last second, he reached out and grabbed her wrist, jerking her down into his arms. Her breasts cushioned against his hard chest, and her legs ended up straddling one of his thick thighs. Instantly her pussy was gushing into her panties, and her blood pressure rose.

He was smiling down at her, with one hand around her back holding her in place, and the other hand holding the cookies out of reach. There was a crumb on his bottom lip and she reached to brush it away before she even realized what she was doing. His eyelids dropped and his tongue came out to lick the tip of her thumb sending a pulse of need rippling through her system.

The sound of Mack clearing his throat broke through the haze of lust and she felt her cheeks heat up as she scrambled to get out of Ryker's lap.

"Sorry, duchess. Tackle first, ask questions later." He didn't look sorry. He looked satisfied and horny all at once.

Turning to face Mack, she hesitated to address what had just happened. Guilt ate at her. She wasn't exactly sure how to explain her desire for his younger brother. If he didn't know how attracted she was to Ryker before, he certainly did now. The worry line splitting his brow in two made her feel like shit.

"Nevermind. I'm not so hungry after all. I think I'll go on in and shower. You boys feel free to enjoy the refreshments and see yourselves out."

She made it to the sliding door before Mack stopped her. He gripped her elbow, but his body lined up nicely with her backside and she groaned as the tingles started all over again.

"Don't worry about it, baby. I'm not upset. Ryker was just playing around. Please sit with us and relax. I want to know more about you."

Her gaze darted back and forth, taking in Mack's attempt at nonchalance, and Ryk's blank expression. The man continued to happily eat her cookies after rocking her to the soles of her feet with just one tumble. Forcing her focus back to Mack, she frowned as she considered all possible outcomes. One misstep would expose her desire for Ryker, and hurt Mack, but she found herself unable to push Ryker away completely either. Something in his feigned indifference reminded her of herself when she was with her father.

Ryker might act like he didn't care what she or Mack thought of him, but deep down he really did. The knowledge hit her like a truck. Ryker needed to be included. Somehow. She wouldn't be content to leave him on the sidelines. Perhaps she fit into Stone River better than she ever expected, because she knew in her heart she craved the pair of them equally.

"I'll give you a cookie if you sit down and play nice." Ryker's statement broke through her emotional turmoil, and she jerked around to stare at him. Meeting her gaze steadily, he shrugged, "Mack will mope for months if you run off now. I didn't realize putting my hands on you upset you so much, duchess, but I'll be more careful in the future."

She had hurt him with her quick retreat from his arms. Somehow the gesture exposed a raw nerve for all three of them. Mack felt pushed aside, she felt caught in the middle, and Ryker felt left out. So how did she go about cementing the three pieces of this puzzle together?

"Your touch didn't upset me. It was you stealing my cookies that did. Don't you know better than to get between a woman and her Oreos?" She moved closer to him as she spoke, and at the last possible second she reached out and scooped up the last couple of cookies from the plate. The grin that split his face relieved the tension in the air, as she took a seat next to him with a sigh of relief

~ ~ ~

Mack watched the byplay between his brother and Claudia with a sense of dread in his throat. Something about the way she looked at Ryker made him nervous. It wasn't that she seemed to want Ryker more, in fact, she looked at Mack with the same amount of longing and desire. It just seemed they were destined to be in a three-way love triangle and there was no way everyone would walk away unscathed. Resigning himself to the possibility of emotional desolation, he took the empty chair next to Claudia, and threw his arm around the back of her chair. If he and his brother were going to compete, then he was going to make damn sure he started with an advantage.

"Mack told me you got cut from your football team for an injury, right?"

The sound of his name drew his attention back to the conversation just in time to see Ryker grimace at the reminder of his situation.

"Damn. Remind me never to steal her cookies again, man. She goes for the jugular right out of the gate." Ryker rubbed a hand over his heart dramatically and then nodded, "Yep that sums it up. I took a hard hit that tore up my shoulder. They had to do surgery on me, and now they won't let me play."

"Why not exactly? I thought football players were injured all the time. Isn't there like a medically unfit list or something?" The combined confusion and genuine interest was adorable on her face. Mack couldn't take his eyes off her. She managed to make eating Oreos look refined and elegant, until she licked the crumbs off her bottom lip. That woke his cock up real quick.

"Injured reserve, and that's only for players who are out for the season, but can come back next season. It allows the team to fill the spot on the roster. Unfortunately when I came out of surgery the doc said my football days were over." Ryker's voice had taken on a hollow haunted tone that warned of impending heavy drinking, and Mack wasn't going to allow it with Claudia around.

"You know, Claudia, I was hoping to take you horseback riding tomorrow if you're free. Maybe we could take some sandwiches and make a day of it? I'd like to show you the ranch." He watched her face closely, but she showed no signs of hesitation when she nodded enthusiastically.

"That would be great! I was going to strip the paint from those shutters, but it can wait for another day. I haven't been on a horse since I was a teenager."

Mack grinned at her excitement, "I was hoping you already knew how to ride."

She tossed her hair, "Damn right I do, cowboy. I wouldn't be a proper Texas girl if I didn't." Wrinkling her nose, she suddenly frowned, "Um, but I haven't ridden a Western saddle since I was little. I rode English."

Ryker snorted, "Let me guess, they didn't think it was proper for a young lady to ride Western? Jesus, your parents must have giant sticks up their—"

"Ryk!" Mack interrupted him with a warning glare.

Claudia just laughed, "It's true. They didn't want their only child to turn out to be a regular cowgirl. I had a great trainer and the best horses to learn on. Lessons were every Friday after ballet."

"You had to ride a horse after dancing all day?" Ryker asked incredulously.

"No, I rode a horse after dancing for a couple of hours. Before ballet was my regular class time with my tutor." Her mirth had shifted into more of a reserved discomfort, but Ryker barreled on.

"Tutor? I can't imagine you struggled in school. You seem pretty damn smart to me, duchess."

A slight sheen of pink blush rose on her cheekbones but she looked him straight in the eye. "No, you're right I didn't have trouble with school. I was homeschooled by private tutors. Another benefit of my parents and their giant sticks."

Ryker seemed to realize his errors and he grimaced, "Sorry, duchess. I didn't mean it the way it sounded."

Interceding, Mack turned to Claudia, "I think it's time for the two of us to head home. Will you come out to the ranch tomorrow about nine? You take the same road out, but instead of turning at the first right, you take the second one. It leads right up to the big house and the stables. I'll meet you there."

"Sounds perfect," she said with a nod as she rose. "I'll have to dig out my riding gear. I'm sure it's packed in a box in the garage."

Ryker started laughing so Mack smacked him on the back of the head. "Sweetheart, you don't need any gear. Jeans and a t-shirt will do just fine for this kind of trail ride."

She hesitated and then nodded, "Of course. I'll manage."

"Don't forget a hat either, duchess. Your skin is too pretty to get burnt up by the sunshine," Ryker said with a wink.

Mack nodded his agreement, and then took her hand in his. "Walk us out?"

She led the way back through the house, but when they reached the front door she hesitated when she pushed the screen door open. Her eyes narrowed on its now silent hinges before she turned and faced them both. "Thank you both for all of your help today. There is no way I would have gotten all of it done without you."

"You're welcome. I hope I'm forgiven for my stupidity last night?" Ryker responded as he walked down the front steps.

"Consider it forgotten," she replied, and the smile he shot her spoke volumes to Mack. There was a plethora of unspoken emotion and longing in his younger brother's eyes, and he didn't know how to respond to it. At this point he couldn't tell him to back off completely because he could see Claudia already cared for him.

A wisp of premonition drifted through his head, and he briefly wondered if they could make a ménage relationship work. He dismissed the idea just as quickly as he recalled Ryker's confusion and irritation at the Keegan wedding. No, a ménage was not in the cards for the Thompson brothers. Something like that would end up turning into World War three and Mack had no desire to see Claudia caught up in the middle of it.

"I'll see you tomorrow morning," he said, brushing a quick kiss over her soft lips. It was tempting to stay and delve deeper into the desire he saw reflected in her hazel eyes, but instead he followed Ryker down the driveway. The two men climbed into their respective vehicles silently, and left Claudia standing on the front porch watching them with a look that held more regret and disappointment than Mack was ready to acknowledge. He could already feel the precarious edge of a cliff under his feet, and he was worried he would fall at any minute.

CHAPTER SIX

Claudia's stomach was a ball of nerves as she drove under the metal scrollwork words "Brooks Pastures" Sunday morning fifteen minutes early. Even though it had been years since she had ridden, it wasn't the horses making her jumpy. Mack made her feel things she wasn't sure she was ready to feel.

When she told him she had kissed Ryker, she assumed he would flip out. Any one of her previous boyfriends would have flown off the handle at the mere suggestion of impropriety with another man, but instead he had laughed it off. Then his reaction to Ryker's affectionate teasing and manhandling of her person had chipped away another layer of her beliefs. She didn't think he was a cuckold. He certainly didn't seem the type of man to get off on watching his girl be used by other men, and yet he didn't react normally to the obvious interest his brother had in her. Trying to wrap her brain around him and Ryker was driving her mad.

A smile broke over her face when the ranch house came into view, and she spotted Mack's broad back next to the barn with two saddled horses ready and waiting. She appreciated his punctuality, and she said so as she climbed out of her car.

His dimples appeared and his blonde curls flashed under the morning sun as he swaggered over to her. She could almost feel his eyes touching every inch of her body when he looked her over. The boots she wore were for hiking instead of riding, but she didn't own a pair of genuine cowboy boots yet, so they would have to do. Otherwise she had settled for a plain white t-shirt and an old pair of jeans. She had tucked her hair up into a beat up ball cap that she kept for yard work, and for the first time in months she wore no make-up. If he was really interested then he may as well see the real Claudia now.

"You look fantastic," he said, reaching for her hand and making her spin for him like a model on the catwalk. "Absolutely delicious."

She tried hard not to blush as she found her center of balance by placing her other hand on his chest, "Thank you. You look pretty damn good yourself this morning."

He wore the same style button down shirt she had seen him in previously, but this one was a well washed blue color that echoed the soft blue of the morning sky. It really made the crystal clear color of his eyes pop, and she couldn't seem to pull her gaze away from his. She knew before he even began to lower his head he was going to kiss her. Some small tick gave him away. Maybe it was a small inhale, or a parting of his lips, or even a flaring of his nostrils, she couldn't be sure which, but she knew.

Fire raced through her from the soft connection between their lips straight to her toes and back centering on her clit, and she moaned into his mouth. His hands slid around her waist and rested on the upper curve of her ass, gently holding her against him while he devastated her with his mouth. His tongue stroked across hers, and his teeth nipped at her bottom lip making her pussy clench. It would be so easy to get lost in his kisses, never to return to reality. He and his brother were made for kissing. The thought of Ryker was like ice water on her heat, and she pulled back, breaking the kiss.

They stared into each other's eyes, panting for breath and imagining the dozens of ways they could get hot and sweaty with each other. Mack's face was slightly flushed with his desire but he stepped back and held his hand out for her to take. He led her to the horses without a word about her pulling away from him, and she felt her walls weakening at his easy acceptance of her limits. She loved that he was equally affected by her, and that he was willing to give her the space when she needed it without questioning her motives.

Forcing her thoughts back to the present, she focused on the pretty mare in front of her, "So who is this?"

"This is Juliet." Mack answered, "And before you ask, yes there is a Romeo in the barn, but he belongs to Parker and I wouldn't put you on his cranky ass for all the kisses in the world."

Claudia stared at him for a moment, before she let out a loud laugh, "Please tell me Rachel and her husbands did not name their daughter after a horse."

He shook his head with a chuckle, "No, not that I know of, but if you decide to ask them please do it when I'm around. I would love to see Parker Brooks' reaction to that question. Now, did you slather up with sunscreen?"

She gave him a funny frown. "Yes, daddy, I did. I might be a city girl, but I'm a smart one."

His laughter died away, and the lust returned to his eyes. "Sweetheart, I promise you I don't feel like your daddy when I'm taking care of you, but if you want to try out a bit of role play sometime I wouldn't be averse. I'm pretty open."

The squeeze of her throat was too tight to talk through, and her tongue suddenly felt too big for her mouth. His wicked suggestion had her panties dripping wet, and she could feel a shiver of excitement skitter through her.

"Horseback riding. That's all we're doing today, cowboy. Focus." She ran her head over the neck of the gentle Juliet, and clucked her tongue at the mare. "Silly men. Only thinking about one thing."

Mack stepped up to her back, and pressed a kiss to the nape of her neck while he rubbed the hard line of his erection against her plump ass. "I'm thinking of lots of things, Claudia, but they all seem to involve you and getting you naked in some form. It's damn hard to concentrate on anything else right now."

"Poor, baby. It's going to hurt riding with that in your pants today," she teased, taking a step to the side to give herself some breathing room. As flattered and turned on as she was by his interest, she still hadn't made him understand that any relationship between the two of them would have to be temporary, and she couldn't live with herself if she led him on and hurt him. "Mack, you know I want you, but I think we need to clear some things up before this goes any farther."

His clear eyes suddenly darkened with confusion, and his body grew tense. "Is this about Ryk?"

"Ryker? What? No! This is about you and me. I'm only in Stone River temporarily. My job won't allow me to live here forever. Once the project is done I have to go back to Austin, or wherever they send me for the next project. I don't want you to be hurt when I leave."

The hint of hostility evaporated and his face relaxed. "Of course. You said so before, but I won't give up trying to convince you to stay. We have something special here, Claudia. A spark I don't imagine too many people feel, and I'm not just talking about the sexual chemistry between us. I want to explore this and see where it leads us, and I really hope you do too."

"Don't get your hopes up, Mack. My life is back in Austin." She stared at the leather saddle covering the back of the horse, doing her best to focus on the tiny engraved lines crisscrossing it in a pretty scrollwork design. It hurt to think of leaving Stone River behind. This was the first place she had ever really felt like she was home. "We'll know more after the town hall meeting. The way I understand it, once everyone has had a chance to say their piece, the town council will take a vote and make a decision. If they veto the project I will have to go home sooner than planned."

The air around them felt heavy, and the horse shuffled a step away from them sensing their tension. She couldn't blame Juliet for wanting to escape it. The last thing Claudia ever wanted to do was fail to secure this project, and have to return home with her tail between her legs.

Instead of arguing or trying to convince her otherwise, Mack just sighed, and resumed his easy going attitude. "Okay. Well then let's just take it one day at a time, shall we? No need worrying about the future until it gets here. Now, up with you city girl, show me how a duchess rides."

Relief washed over her, along with a touch of annoyance at his use of the prissy nickname. "Just because I rode in an arena doesn't mean I don't have skills, cowboy. Back up." She gave him a little shove with her shoulder to his ribs, and lifted her foot into the stirrup. The swing up into the saddle was high, but she felt at ease once she took her seat. There was something comforting about the easy acceptance of Juliet, and the gentle sway of her movements as she adjusted to Claudia's weight. The saddle felt different than she was used to, but not terribly so, and she quickly took the reins to direct the mare away from the barn. Glancing over her shoulder at Mack, she smiled saucily, "You coming, cowboy? Or are you just going to watch me show you how it's done?"

His laughter boomed through the yard, echoing off the building and drawing a couple of ranch hands out of the barn. The front door of the house opened, and Rachel stepped outside holding a chubby little girl in her arms. The man who followed her onto the porch looked a lot like Sawyer, and the possessive way his arm wrapped around the two females with him, assured her this was another Brooks brother.

"Claudia! It's good to see you again," Rachel called out, and Claudia directed the horse over to the edge of the porch to greet her new friend.

"You too, Rachel, and this must be your lovely Juliet."

Juliet was sucking on her fist like it was the last bit of food in the world. Drool coated the one-year-old's chin and chest, but the smile she gave her mom when her name was mentioned was radiant. "Yes, this is Miss Jules, and this is my husband, Hudson, I don't think you two have met yet."

Claudia nodded at Hudson Brooks, wondering again how Rachel managed to juggle so many men in her life. Just being with Mack and Ryker as a pair left her feeling out of her element, so she couldn't imagine how much harder it would be if she were dating them both.

"Nice to meet you, Claudia," Hudson said politely. "You're not quite what I pictured when Sawyer told me Mack was dating a real estate tycoon."

Shaking her head, she laughed, "I'm no real estate tycoon. Just a regular woman doing a job. With any luck the town will side with Schmidt Properties tomorrow night and Granite Estates will be a reality."

"Exactly why would that be a good thing?" Another Brooks brother appeared in the doorway, and Claudia actually felt herself cringe away from the distrust and genuine disgust he directed her way.

"Rogan, stop it. Be polite," Rachel snapped.

Refusing to cower, Claudia stiffened her spine and leveled her gaze on Rogan Brooks. "Mr. Brooks, Granite Estates would bring more families to Stone River, which at this moment is bogged down in the good old days. The world has changed, but this tiny Texas town has resisted changing with it. It can't hold out forever. If not Schmidt, then another company will come in and buy up land, but instead of putting up homes and schools, and bringing in businesses, they will throw up oil derricks and trailer parks for the workers who run them."

"Not if we stand our ground," Rogan snapped. "The last thing we need is for Austin to swallow up Stone River. We live here because we like being part of a small town. If you bring the city here it will take away our freedom, and the values we have built generations of families on. I don't dislike you, Ms. Schmidt. I don't know you. But in all fairness, you don't know me either. So how can you be so sure this development is what's best for me and my family?"

Her argument died on her tongue when Rogan reached out and took Juliet from Rachel's arms. He held the little girl against his chest, uncaring when she drooled all over his shoulder, gumming his shirt. This wasn't a council member, or a protester. This was a man with a family, and an idea. Even if it was naïve, he believed there was room in the world for small towns and slow easy lifestyles.

"Out of respect for you and your family, I think we should agree to disagree. Today is my day off, and I would prefer not to debate the morality of my job if it's all the same to you," she offered. "It was nice to meet you all."

Turning her head, she realized Mack was already astride his horse and waiting just behind her. He appeared to be ruminating over their conversation, and he wore a deep frown until he caught her eye. Giving her a wink, he waved to the Brooks family, "We'll be out all day. I want to show her the ranch, and the pond."

"You two have fun," Rachel responded enthusiastically.

"We'll see you at the town hall meeting, Ms. Schmidt. Enjoy your ride." Rogan gave her a nod, and she was sure that was as close to a truce as she was going to get. Clearly the town planning board wasn't the only hurdle standing in the way of this project.

Following Mack out of the yard, she chewed on all of the information she knew about Stone River. It was settled in the early eighteen hundreds by the Raft family who set up a trading post and made nice with the local Native Americans. It had never really been a boom town like many other places, so it hadn't ever fallen into disrepair as most ghost towns did after their heyday. Instead, a handful of families had planted their roots here, and built up a close-knit community who valued a good day's work, and honest living.

From what she had seen with Rachel's family it was obvious Stone River was an accepting group of people. They clearly valued a person's heart more than their sexual proclivities. Mack had even mentioned a BDSM club nearby. Perhaps this was a case of still waters running deep. There seemed to be much more to this tiny town than she ever could have imagined, and now she felt like her alliances were being torn apart.

On one side stood her father and his life's blood—Schmidt Properties, and on the other side were the people of Stone River who were accepting her and embracing her in every way except business. She had no desire to change the town, or shift their ideals. She just wanted her father to accept her as an equal, and stop treating her like a teenager whining over her zits and gossiping about her date to the prom. If she was ever going to be taken seriously as his heir to the position of CEO, then she had no choice but to push this project on the people of Stone River. No matter what her personal feelings were. It just didn't sit right.

"You're awfully deep in thought for a woman who's supposed to be enjoying her day off with a relaxing trail ride," Mack said, and she looked up, startled to find they had traveled far enough she couldn't see the Brooks family home anymore. They were surrounded by a sea of rolling hills and thick green and yellow grasses. In some areas the grass was knee-high to the horses who grazed on it. She couldn't imagine a sight more magnificent than the peaceful serenity of this Texas ground.

"Wow. It's so pretty here," she declared. "This is all Brooks land?"

"Mmmhmm. They've owned it for decades the way I understand it."

"How long have you known the Brooks family?" she asked, adjusting her seat in the saddle. The horse had a pleasantly even gait, but the slope of the saddle was just different enough from what she was used to that she felt a little awkward in her seat.

"I met Parker probably eight years ago when I owned my own business. He was a customer of mine, and we hit it off as friends," Mack

66

explained. She admired the grace he and his horse had together. A symbiotic relationship that appeared to be completely fluid and fulfilling for both man and horse. And he looked damn hot in the saddle with a cowboy hat pulled low over his brow, his trademark red bandana peeking out from underneath.

Jerking in the saddle, she fought to remember what their conversation had been about as her hormones dominated her thought process again. What was it about this man that sent her hurdling off the cliff of reason just being close?

"You had a business?" The subtle way he dropped the fact into conversation but didn't elaborate wasn't lost on her, but she wanted to know more about his life pre-cowboy days. "What kind of business?"

They'd reached the edge of an oval shaped pond surrounded on three sides by trees. A fire pit and a dock dominated one end of the pool, and she could imagine many a campfire late into the night with the smell of wood-smoke and burnt marshmallows heavy on the air. Mack stopped his horse and faced her, meeting her eyes before he answered her question.

"At one time in my life I was a Master leather artisan. I ran my own company, Saddle-Up Leather. I created all kinds of things out of leather. Saddles, bags, belts…even floggers and harnesses for BDSM players." He sounded both proud and wistful about his past, "I was making money hand over fist for years, but as good as I was with leather, I was equally bad with business. I chose the wrong employees, the money was mismanaged, bills weren't paid on time. It was a disaster of monumental proportions and the business collapsed underneath me."

"You loved it though." It wasn't a question, and she didn't expect an answer. She could see on his face and in his eyes how much he missed working his craft. "Would you show me some of your work sometime?"

His face split into a wide grin, "Sure. Look down. You're sitting on one of my saddles."

She felt her mouth drop open, and she heard her gasp of surprise, but she didn't remember sliding out of the saddle and dropping to the ground to inspect it closer. Her fingers traced the deep grooves in the supple leather, and she wondered out loud how many hours something like that would take.

"An intricate one like this can take up to forty man hours. A simpler design I can have done in thirty. It just depends. Saddles are where I got my start. My father enjoyed creating them, and taught me everything he knew when he realized I had a knack for it."

Meeting his eyes after he climbed off his own mount, she smiled up at him, "You do amazing work on saddles, Mr. Thompson, but I must admit to being curious about the other items you listed. How does one go about making harnesses and floggers?"

"Hmm, well for that kind of explanation I would really need to give you a demonstration, and that's not going to happen today. Just suffice it to say I've learned what sells the best over the years by testing them in my hand and even on my own body." His nonchalant way of stating his experience left her open mouthed again.

"You let someone flog you?" she asked. "But I thought you were into BDSM because you liked to flog women?"

Her question seemed to stop him in his tracks as he worked his brain to come up with a suitable response. His jaw tightened and relaxed more than once and his throat worked as he swallowed hard. "BDSM isn't just about men hitting women. It's never about abuse if it's practiced correctly. I'm not much for inflicting pain, but it turns me on a lot to have control over another person's pleasure. I'm Dominant ninety percent of the time, but I've also walked on the other side of the line. I'm what they call a Switch. I can switch back and forth between Dominating and submitting and still find my pleasure, but I lean toward the Dominant side."

She let him lead her down the slope of the hill into the trees and over to the bank of the creek, barely noticing the saddlebags he carried until he was spreading picnic accruements on the grassy edge. He pulled out plates, silverware, and napkins, before bringing out a half dozen sandwiches, potato salad, and watermelon wedges. "This is your idea of a few sandwiches?"

"I wanted to make sure you weren't hungry. Riding is a workout when you're not used to it. Eat up." He passed her a bottle of water and a plate and she helped herself to the food. Bacon, lettuce, and tomato sandwiches were one of her favorite summer foods, and she moaned as she inhaled her first sandwich.

"This is delicious. Did you make all of this?"

He nodded looking slightly uncomfortable at her praise, "It's not a big deal, just something quick to fill the grumbly hole up. Did I make you uncomfortable with all of that BDSM talk?"

Claudia hesitated before she answered thinking her response out. "No, not really. I'm curious, not put off. When you're being Dominant what exactly does that mean?"

"It depends on who I'm with." She flinched at the reminder that he would have to have had a partner to explore BDSM with, and he frowned at her. "I'm not a priest, Claudia. I'm thirty-five years old. I've been with other women."

A hot flush crept up her cheeks. "I know. I just don't like thinking about the other women you've been with."

He gave her a blinding smile that highlighted his perfectly straight teeth and deep dimples. "You're jealous? Good, then we're making progress."

"You want me to be jealous?" she asked in confusion.

Shaking his head, he laughed, "Not necessarily, but if you are it means you care. And I definitely want you to care, sweetheart."

He dropped a kiss on her lips but pulled away before she could deepen it. His lips were like crack and she felt like an addict. Just one taste and she was a goner. "Back to the point, what does Dominant mean to you?"

Pushing her plate away, she relaxed into the grass, resting on her side as she waited for him to answer. To her surprise he seemed completely comfortable talking about the subject.

"I prefer to be in control in my relationships for the most part. Not in the sense I need to micromanage my partner's every waking moment—that would be a Master/slave relationship and it's not appealing to me. Instead I like to know that if she needs something she will look to me to provide it. Whether it be comfort after a long day, a sounding board for her daily life, or mind-numbing pleasure all night long. I want to be the central focus of her life as much as she is mine, but I want her to trust me to make decisions for her benefit."

"So you want a mindless twit you can boss around?" she asked. Her tone was righteous and indignant, but everything she knew about BDSM could be held on a tablespoon, and he wasn't exactly making it any more appealing.

"Not at all. In fact, I prefer a partner and completely open communication. You have to be able to have an intelligent conversation with your partner, otherwise what's the point? No, most of my Dominant tendencies appear in the bedroom, and in my over-protective nature." He finished packing away their lunch, and stretched out on the grass beside her. Once he was settled he held out his arm, indicating that she could scoot closer. Her head settled into the crook of his shoulder, and his masculine fragrance filled her nose, addling her brain. "I find it hard to explain what I want out of a partner, because there's a small part of me that gets a thrill out of allowing a woman to take temporary control in bed too. I'm not averse to a bit of bondage in my bed, even if it's me being tied down."

She could hear the blood rushing through her ears and her heart pounding as she tried not to give herself away. It wasn't time for him to know how much his fantasy turned her on. The bedroom was the only place she ever seemed to be in control, and it scared her he might ask her to give it up completely. Her whole life was dictated by someone else. It always had been. So when she started dating, she found herself selecting men who were easily directed. Men who were on the doormat side of pushover, and none of her relationships lasted very long. Just because she wanted to take over in bed on occasion didn't mean she didn't want a man who could be a real man in other aspects of their relationship.

"You're thinking an awful lot. This is supposed to be relaxing," Mack said, and she tipped her head to find him watching her.

"You're giving me a lot to think about. I guess I've always assumed people were either Dominant or submissive. Not both. I'm not sure how it can work, but I'm intrigued."

He dropped a kiss on her nose with a chuckle. "Good, I can work with intrigued. So tell me about yourself."

She snorted, "I'm pretty boring."

Poking her in the side, he growled a little. "So tell me the boring basics. What's your middle name?"

"Dawn. Claudia Dawn Schmidt. What's yours?"

"Granger." He rolled his eyes when she frowned in question, "It was my mom's maiden name. I'm Cormac Granger Thompson."

"Cormac?"

Nodding, he explained, "My father's mother was Irish, and he and my mother wanted to honor her heritage. I hated the name as a kid, so everyone called me Mack."

"I like Cormac, but Mack seems to suit you better. What's Ryker's middle name?"

"Denver. It's where he was born. Mom and Dad had a trip to the mountains planned for their fifth wedding anniversary. Mom was seven months pregnant and she fell getting out of the cab at the hotel. It sent her into labor, and she never even made it to the mountain. Ryk was born small because he was early, so he and mom had to stay in Denver for a few weeks before she could bring him home."

"Wow! I never would have imagined Ryker would have started out premature. He certainly grew up," she said with a laugh. Her laughter died when she realized Mack had gone tense underneath her. Rising up on her elbows, she looked down into his face. "What? What's wrong?"

"Do you like Ryker, Claudia?" he asked bluntly.

"Of course I like him, Mack. Why are you asking?"

Shaking his head, he gave her a concerned frown, "No, I mean do you *like* like him?"

Her eyes were rolling before he even got the whole question out of his mouth, "Are you fucking kidding me? What's next, a note that says check yes or no? We're not in junior high, Mack. Spit it out."

In an instant she found herself on her back, with Mack sprawled over her. His large frame pinning her to the soft grass, with his hips wedged between her thighs. Her wrists were held loosely above her head in one of his massive hands, while the other hand gripped her hair, holding her in place.

Dilated pupils and flaring nostrils told her he wasn't joking when he snarled down at her. "You know what I mean, sweetheart. Do you want to fuck, Ryker? Do you want his cock in your pussy, fucking you, claiming you? I know you want me. I see it in your eyes, and I smell it on the air every time you get close to me. So tell me the truth. Do you want Ryker just as much?"

Air pumped out of her lungs wickedly fast as she tried to contain her rising lust. Between his body position, his angry possessiveness, and his dirty talk she was ready to fuck without another word, but it wouldn't help this situation.

"Yes. Damn it. I'm attracted to Ryker. His kiss turned me on, and I've thought about him. I'm sorry if it hurts you, Mack, but it's the God's honest truth. I won't lie to you."

She watched him apprehensively; terrified he would pull away from her now that she had admitted her attraction to Ryker. Instead, his fingers clenched tighter around her ponytail, and he rocked forward, grinding his erection against the inflamed V of her thighs and making her moan out loud.

"Thank you for being honest. Now, I'll be honest with you. I don't think Ryker and I are built the same way the Brooks brothers are, or the Keegan brothers are. I can't see us sharing a house for much longer, much less a woman. We're two very different people, and I understand your attraction to him. All I'm asking is that you let me show you how good it can be between the two of us, before you decide if you want to pursue Ryker." Worry filled his eyes, but it was tempered by his desire. He had amazing self-control because she was ready to self-combust.

It took her several tries, but she managed to squeak out, "Yes."

A satisfied smirk lit up his features before his mouth dropped to hers, and he began his seduction. As his kiss branded her lips, she felt it leave a permanent mark on her heart too. He may not realize it yet, but she had already given her heart to him. The only catch was his younger brother had a grip on it too.

~ ~ ~

Mack couldn't believe his good fortune. Not only did he find a woman who was beautiful, intelligent, and kind hearted, but she seemed to genuinely care about him as a person. Since he declared bankruptcy on his life's work, and walked away from Saddle-Up, he had avoided dating. It was completely out of character for him to walk up to a woman and ask her out, but with Claudia it seemed natural. Something about her hooked him in from the moment he heard the whiskey notes of her voice, and spotted her lush curves. He wanted her with every fiber of his being, but the scary part was he already knew he needed her too. Three days shouldn't have been enough to feel that way, but somehow it was.

Her heat poured into him via their kiss, scorching his soul and stealing his breath. It was intoxicating, and he felt his balls tighten as she shifted against him. Her body undulated as much as she could in the small space underneath him, and she let out a whimper of need that cut through to his core. Breaking their kiss, he nipped her bottom lip.

"Tell me no, Claudia. Tell me to stop now or I'll keep going until I have you begging for my cock." He held back a laugh at the flash of indignation that battled with desire in her eyes.

The corners of her sweetly swollen lips curved up slightly and her pink tongue darted out to wet them before she whispered, "I don't beg, Mack, so do your worst."

The dare was too much to resist when he already wanted her so much. His blood hummed through his body, so strong was his craving for her. He could see his own need reflected back to him in her eyes, and it intensified every caress of their bodies, every touch of their skin.

With a slight shift of his hips, he seated himself more firmly between her thighs, pressing the length of his erection against the molten core between her legs. The pressure of her heels against the back of his knees sent a shiver up his spine. Her hands curls up around the back of his neck, tugging him back down to her and mashing their mouths together until they shared the same breath. She became the oxygen his blood needed.

Sliding one hand up her torso under her t-shirt, he tweaked the hard bud of a nipple under the satin cover of her bra. Forcing her to release his neck, he shimmied down her body making sure to add more pressure to the V between her legs than necessary. She delighted him by groaning and arching her back, lifting her breasts up to his mouth in a decadent offering fit for the Gods. Later he wouldn't remember tugging her shirt off, or snapping the strap of her bra, but somehow it happened, and her luscious tits were bare to his mouth.

Claudia's gasps grew in intensity as he suckled, squeezed, pinched, and bit at the perfect globes. They overflowed his hands, and he knew someday he wanted to squeeze them tightly around his cock, watching them swallow him up. Every inch of skin that appeared as he pushed her skin tight jeans over her soft thighs was deliciously perfect. She had broad hips he knew served as the platform for a plump heart shaped ass that would cradle him nicely. Her tummy was soft, and her belly button deep, and he proceeded to taste them as he made his way down the valley of her torso to the curl topped mound of glory between her legs.

Her desire glistened on the blonde curls, and he inhaled her musky scent deep into his lungs, knowing he would never forget this moment. Listening to her mewling with pleasure from his work roughened hands, and watching her rise to feel his hot breath on her skin, left him feeling primal. It was all he could do to keep from lifting up and plunging into her hot cunt in one long brutal stroke.

"Mack! Stop teasing me," she groaned when he blew his breath out across the pearly pink head of her clit.

Chuckling, he winked at her from his place on his belly between her legs. "Mmm...not quite begging yet. A little less sass next time, sweetheart, and maybe I'll give in."

Before she could snipe back at him, he dropped his head, and using his thumb and forefinger, he spread the swollen lips of her labia, getting his first view of heaven. Like a red cape to a bull, her pink slit called to him, and his mouth watered to love her. Magic burst on his tongue at the first taste of her sweet cream. The stiff nub of her clit making his tongue tingle, and his balls draw up tight. He heard her squeal of pleasure, and then her muttered pleas of mercy as he ran his tongue from top to bottom and back before sinking into her tight hole.

Sweet Jesus, she was tight. Her pussy muscles gripped his tongue, sucking and pulling on it as though to keep it in place. Instead he alternated fucking her with it and running it in tight gentle circles around her clit. Just when she would begin to tremble under him, he would pull back and blow a cold breath over her sizzling skin. It wasn't long before he had to dig his fingers into her hips to hold her thrusting hips down. When she finally began begging it was a relief to his stubborn pride and his aching cock.

"Mack, please, please, please!"

Her pretty plea turned him on more than she would ever know, and he gripped his now bare cock with his hand trying to stave off the impending orgasm he could feel in his nuts.

She shocked him further by grabbing ahold of his throbbing dick and flipping their positions. Rising up over him, she looked up at him through her lashes, and licked the crown of his cock with her scorching hot tongue. He could feel sweat pop up on his upper lip as he hissed out his appreciation for her sweet affection. The soft cavern of her mouth was absolutely perfect, and feeling the back of her throat against his tip made his heart skip a beat. She bobbed on him for a few minutes, giving him the best damn head he'd ever experienced, without even deep-throating him.

Her hand moved up and down in time with her mouth, so he didn't even care that she was only swallowing the first three or four inches. And then she added a little twisting motion to her grip and he nearly shot off into her mouth.

Gripping her biceps, he tugged her up his body and rolled her onto her back again before she had a chance to protest. "That's all I can take, sweetheart. If I don't get inside of you I'll explode. Open for me."

Instantly she slid her legs higher up his hips, opening her pussy up to his searching cock. It was a tight fit, but he managed to line them up and ease the head of his dick into her sweet honey hole. The scent of arousal and grass surrounded them as he slowly fucked his way deep into her. She gave as good as she got, rocking her hips up to meet his pounding thrusts, gripping his biceps as they flexed with his movements. Her nails dug into his skin, giving him an added layer of pain that kept him from blowing his load too quickly.

It wasn't long before they had both lost all illusion of control, and were just madly thrusting against each other, his cock slamming into her cervix with every motion, and her wild cries echoing through the trees around them. She screamed out her climax so loudly it triggered his orgasm. He pressed his groin as tightly to her as possible, flexing his cock inside of her as her muscles milked his cum from him.

Hot, sweaty, and sated, they rested there together, temporarily connected, and somehow permanently changed. It was several minutes before Mack was able to lift his head from her chest to meet her gaze, and he felt immeasurably pleased with himself when he saw the exhaustion on her face.

"See, begging isn't so bad," he whispered, laughing when she smacked his chest with a crack of her palm.

Narrowing her eyes, she gave him a push, "Turnabouts fair play, Mr. Thompson, and I plan on making you squeal like a little girl when I get a chance. Now up with you, we need to clean up. I'm pretty sure there is a small stick permanently embedded in my right ass cheek."

Shame washed through him, and he cringed as he rose. "I'm sorry, Claudia. I shouldn't have taken you like that, but I didn't have it planned."

The smile on her face was relaxed, "I know, Mack. If I thought any different it wouldn't have happened, but it turns out I wanted you just as much as you wanted me."

He helped her up onto her feet and then spun her around. Grass and dirt marred her sexy back and ass, and he felt terrible. "I'm no better than an animal, ripping your clothes off and fucking you in the dirt. I wouldn't blame you if you hated me."

To his surprise she giggled, and then grabbed his now deflated cock making it twitch with new life. "You think I could hate you after that? Do you know how sexy you made me feel? Just knowing how much you wanted me, and yet you delayed your own pleasure for mine. And besides, you just gave me my first orgasm via actual sex."

"I—what?" Mack knew he looked like a fool standing there with his pants around his hips open, cock hanging out, and now mouth hanging open.

"Yep. I've had orgasms that were self-induced, and once with an ex when he used a vibrator, but never in the act. So you better make sure the notch in your bedpost is a deep one cowboy, because I don't plan on this being a onetime occurrence."

"I'm all yours, anytime you want me, Claudia."

With a sexy wink she sashayed away swinging her curvy hips. He didn't even manage to get another word out before she dove into the pond and reemerged like a mermaid calling out to a sailor. Her breasts bobbed on the water, and her hair spread out around her like a cape. "What are you waiting for? I told you we needed to clean up."

He didn't wait for another moment. Laughing all the way, he stripped his clothes off and joined his mermaid in the water. Never before had he felt so accepted or wanted for himself. Love filled the void in his soul he hadn't even known he had. Now he just needed to figure out the best way to keep her in Stone River.

CHAPTER SEVEN

Claudia wrapped a towel around her wet body as she ran to answer the front door the next afternoon. She wasn't expecting to find Mack standing there but she readily returned his friendly smile and hello kiss when she opened the door.

"What are you doing here? Why aren't you working?" she asked, pushing the door shut, and tightening her grip on the towel.

"I took off early. I wanted to see you again, and if I had known you would be naked and wet I would have taken the morning off too," he said with a wicked glint in his eyes, reaching for her towel as she darted away.

"I was supposed to have dinner with Mayor Edwards tonight to discuss the project, but he backed out about an hour ago without rescheduling," she responded, with a heavy sigh.

Mack frowned, "That can't be a good sign."

"I'm not beaten yet. If he thinks avoiding dinner with me will get me off the trail, he's mistaken."

Mack's dimples flashed as he smiled at her, and she reached up to run her finger over one of the deep grooves. Turning his head, he captured her fingertip with his lips and nipped her gently. "So does this mean you're free to spend the rest of the day with me?"

"I suppose so. As long as you don't suggest going for another trail ride," she said, grimacing as she rubbed at her tender backside.

Instantly, concern filled his gaze and his eyes narrowed, "Are you hurt? I shouldn't have kept you out so long yesterday. It's been too long since you were in the saddle." He grabbed her arm and tugged her toward the stairs, "Damn it. I wish I had known, I could have brought some liniment to rub on your muscles."

"Mack, stop!" she protested, but he continued to pull her along up the stairs, only hesitating long enough for her to direct him to the right bedroom. Before she could get her bearings he was pushing her down on the bed and pulling her towel away. "Hey!"

A sharp slap to the side of her hip made her squeal in surprise. "I want to make sure you're not bruised. Spread 'em."

He pushed her thighs apart, and she felt moisture flood her pussy as he ran his hands up and down her inner thighs and over her plump ass. "Mmm. I won't protest if you deem a massage is in order," she teased.

The tentative touches became firmer and he chuckled behind her. "Have I mentioned how much I like your dirty talking side?"

Rolling up on her side, she rested her head on her hand and gave him what she hoped was a seductive look. "How about this side? Are you interested in this side too?"

The heat lighting up his eyes made her skin tingle. His breathing was heavier as she whispered, "Definitely. Roll over, sweetheart, so I can play with those pretty tits."

Shaking her head, she rolled over but she didn't stay put. "Nope. I think it's my turn to make you squeal. Remember? I've got some scarves I think I'm going to use on you just to ensure you can't take over."

Shock filled his features, and a pink flush stained his cheeks, but she saw his cock twitch with interest behind the denim of his jeans. His body suddenly tensed and he took a step backwards. Jumping to her feet, she placed one hand on his chest, and gripped the back of his neck with the other, drawing his eyes back to hers. "Hey! Why are you so embarrassed?"

"I'm not," he argued, but she wouldn't release him when he tried to pull away. "I'm fine, really."

"No, wait, if we're going to pursue this relationship you have to talk to me. Why are you suddenly acting awkward? Is it because I want to tie you up?"

Mack slowly shook his head, and took a deep breath. "No. It's because I want you to. I'm not entirely comfortable with my desire to be on the receiving end yet."

"We'll take it slow. Practice makes perfect, right? I'm assuming you would like the opportunity to tie my ass up and drive me insane." She lifted an eyebrow at him, and giggled when his grin widened. "That's what I thought. Well fair's fair. I want to explore this gorgeous piece of man-flesh, and the only way to prevent you from taking over is to tie you down. Are you game?"

"Man-flesh?" He looked genuinely affronted at her choice of words and she rolled her eyes.

"Seriously? Are you in or not?"

Mack suddenly laughed loudly and wrapped his arms around her middle, pulling her up onto her toes so he could kiss her. When they parted to breathe again, he smiled down at her. "You're perfect, do you know that?"

"Of course I am. Now, on your back, cowboy. I'm going to lasso you." She wiggled her eyebrows and bounced over to her dresser to pull out several silk scarves that would bind him securely to the headboard. *Hopefully they won't leave marks*, she thought. The moment the thought crossed her brain she smiled inside at the image of another woman seeing her marks on his wrists. Pure feminine pride filled her chest, and she stalked back to the bed, determined to leave a mark on his soul, if not his body. She wanted to rock him to the core like he did her yesterday.

Straddling his chest, she tied his wrists and then scratched her nails lightly down his forearms to the tender skin on the inside of his arms. Goosebumps popped up all over his skin, and she continued her exploration over his shoulders and neck, tangling her fingers in his yellow curls.

"I love your hair. It's so sexy. You should leave the bandana off more often," she murmured, pressing tiny butterfly kisses to his forehead and cheeks.

His lips parted, but he didn't respond, and she continued to kiss every inch of skin she could reach. Making her way down to his broad chest, she nipped at the tan circles of his nipples making him twist underneath her. She filed away the knowledge that his nipples were sensitive as she moved on to the sharp jut of his rib cage. There was a scar over his left bottom rib and she traced the four inch line with her tongue.

"What happened?" she whispered against his skin.

He shuddered underneath her, and his voice was thick with desire when he answered, "A tree branch when I was nine. I was climbing a tree and slipped. I caught the edge of a broken branch as I went down. Got lucky it didn't go through me."

Pressing another tender kiss to the old wound, she moved on to his rock hard abs, flexing beneath her hot breath. The line of hair stretching down his center intrigued her. It was crisp under her fingers, but soft against her skin, and it led her further down his body until she came face to face with his thick cock. Easily eight inches long and thick, she was fascinated by the thick vein running along its underside, pulsing with his heartbeat.

Her tongue followed the line up to the dripping hole at the top, and then back down to the especially sensitive spot where his cock and sack connected. Heavy balls hung below his shaft, begging for her hands, and she didn't hesitate to run her lips over them, before rolling them in her palm. Mack was moaning now, his thighs tense on either side of her head as she fondled him.

Watching his face closely, she engulfed the head of his cock with her mouth while twisting and tugging ever so gently at his nuts. His hips jerked upwards and she smiled around the mouthful of cock. Taking another chance, she scratched her fingertip over the sensitive purse of his anus while she swallowed as much of his cock as possible.

The wild way he twisted and jumped encouraged her to press her fingertip harder against his pleasure button, just barely entering him on the next swallow. Still, he didn't protest. In fact, his pupils dilated and a pink flush covered his chest and cheeks, proving how much he was enjoying her attentions. Before she could second guess herself, she pushed her finger into his ass, and forced another inch of his cock into her throat, gagging just a bit. The spurt of pre-cum that filled her mouth left her gurgling for air, and she had to release him.

When she lifted her head again, he looked like a wild man. His biceps were bulging, and his abs were clenched. His cockhead was an angry purple color, and he growled at her when she didn't immediately resume her fondling.

"I need to be inside you, baby. Now." He was gritting his teeth as he tried to maintain control, and Claudia frowned down at him.

"I'm the boss today, *baby*. So relax. I'm going to ride you, but it's going to be slow and easy," she assured him as she rose up over his hips and lined his cock up with her dripping snatch. Slowly she sunk down on him, taking a couple of thrusts to get him all the way inside of her.

They came together like a match to kindling. Fire coursed through her veins, making her motions jerky and sharp. Mack groaned underneath her when she leaned forward dragging her aching nipples over his mouth.

"I would die happy if I suffocate with my face full of those beauties," he hissed at her, and she giggled. "Let my hands loose, sweetheart. I want to touch you."

Claudia hesitated, because she was enjoying having control, but if she was honest, it wasn't nearly as sexy to ride his cock without him holding her. Hurrying to release the ties, she had to stretch almost the full length of her body on top of him to reach them. The moment his hands were free, he gripped her hips, his fingertips digging into the soft flesh, hard enough to leave bruises. She screamed when he shoved his cock upwards, spearing her hard and fast. An orgasm washed over her, leaving her lying limply on top of him, trying to remember why this was a bad idea in the first place.

Mack might have stayed on his back, but he definitely took control. Moving her hips to a rhythm that quickly brought them both back to the edge of orgasm. With her last bit of functioning brain cells, she reached out and pinched his nipples as she exploded on top of him. Whimpering and babbling her pleasure as he released his cum deep inside of her.

She collapsed onto him, her vision slightly fuzzy, and her body tingling everywhere. There was no denying they were explosive together. Lying there in blissful silence, she listened to his heart race under her ear and just breathed in the scent of sex as he ran his fingers up and down her spine gently.

"I hate to ruin the moment, but this is the second time we've had sex and the second time we've forgotten a condom," Mack said hesitantly.

Claudia turned her head, so her chin rested over his breastbone and she could meet his eyes. "I'm clean, and safe from pregnancy. I have an IUD, but I should have been more responsible. To be honest, I don't sleep with just anyone. I haven't had sex in over a year."

He hugged her tightly, and pulled her up to kiss her forehead. "I'm clean too, but I'll get you papers if you'd like to see. I haven't had a serious relationship since right before the business went under. When I slept with a sub at The Cage there was always a condom involved."

She nodded, "I'll get paperwork for you too." Frowning, she wrinkled her nose, "Not very sexy talk for after something like that."

"No, but I wanted to make sure you were protected." He cocked his head, "I want to be a dad, but not until I have my life pieced back together."

Lifting off him, she went to the bathroom to clean up and then rejoined him in her bed. Snuggling up to his naked body, she relaxed on his shoulder and let her eyes drift closed listening to him breathe.

"Mack? When you say you want to piece your life back together, what does that mean exactly?" she asked quietly, unsure if he was still awake or not.

After several breaths she decided he must have fallen asleep and she sighed heavily, jumping when his voice startled her, "I really don't know. I've just kind of been hanging on by the skin of my teeth for the last few years. No sense of direction or purpose. I guess I'm hoping things will start to fall in place for me soon."

"I know what you mean." Before drifting off to sleep, she allowed herself to imagine she had found a permanent home in Stone River, and possibly the missing puzzle pieces to her empty life.

~ ~ ~

Ryker didn't know what drew him back to Claudia, but for whatever reason he found himself back at her home, scraping paint from the east side of the house. She turned out to be an easy person to talk to, and he found himself sharing all of the sordid details of his past with Tina and Scott.

"So, Scott had been working as your accountant for five years and he had been honest the whole time?" she asked. The confusion in her voice matched the questions he'd been asking himself for months.

"Yep. Not a penny out of place until I hired Tina Ash as my business manager. I was looking into opening a bar and grill in Galveston before my football contract was due to end in two years. I figured I had better start making plans for a future that didn't involve full body contact."

"And the police can't do anything? What about tracking the money electronically? Surely the bank knows where it was sent. My father had an incident with an employee embezzling a decade ago, but they managed to piece together the missing money and arrest him."

Ryker shook his head as he climbed back down the ladder and joined her under the shade of the neighbor's Maple tree draping over part of her yard. "The positive and negative about technological improvements. They sent the money to overseas accounts, and then began a series of complicated transfers. Apparently Tina was a hacker in her juvy days. Of course, that was a fact she conveniently left off her resume."

"I'll bet. I know it sucks, but Karma will bite them in the ass someday, Ryker."

The look of concern in her pretty hazel eyes made his heart clench. "Thanks. I know you're right. It just sucks to lose everything in a matter of days."

"But Mack said you sold your home and some cars, so you should have a nice nest egg, right?"

"I have enough. I don't have to work as a ranch hand like Mack." He didn't mean it the way it sounded, and she bristled.

"At least he's not sitting in a recliner feeling sorry for himself, and crying into a can of beer." Her words created an awkward silence between the two of them, and he had to bite back a nasty response because the truth hurt.

"Well played. I'm sorry. It's just a sensitive subject. I have to figure out what's next for me." Ryker watched as her eyes suddenly stared off and her tone grew distant.

"Yeah, there seems to be a lot of that going on around here."

Before he could question her more, her cell phone rang and she hurried to answer it. He heard her greet one of the town board members and confirm her attendance at the town hall meeting later that night. He was actually anxious to see her in action. The image of her in his head didn't match up to the rich socialite he knew she had been before moving to Stone River.

When she hung up and walked back his way, he gestured to the phone, "Getting nervous?"

"No, not really. Well, no more nervous than I was before. The town is certainly determined to hold off development. I just hope they keep an open mind tonight."

"Give them a little credit. Just because they live in the sticks doesn't mean they aren't open minded. They do seem to embrace alternative lifestyles..." he said, wiggling his eyebrows at her and making her laugh.

"That they do. I have to admit, that part of Stone River caught me off guard."

Ryker nodded his agreement. "Me too. I was at the Keegan wedding, and I saw how much the three brothers love Zoey with my own eyes, but it still seems weird to me. I mean, how do they decide things like who goes on the marriage license, or who goes to parent/teacher conferences with the kids?"

Claudia looked thoughtful, and she absently rubbed sweat from her cleavage distracting Ryker and making his cock twitch. "I suppose it takes a lot of communication. Who did Zoey legally marry?"

"It's Tanner's signature on the doc. He's the oldest, and the legal owner of the ranch, but she said vows with all three of them."

"I wish I could have been there. I love weddings, and I've been to a hundred or more. Big ones, small ones, weird ones...I went to one where the theme of the wedding was *Nightmare Before Christmas*, and the bride and groom dressed up as Jack and Sally. I've never seen a bride marry more than one groom, though."

Ryker grinned, "Like I said, small town doesn't mean small minded." He passed her a bottle of water, watching as she drank deeply. When she dropped it from her lips, her sexy pink tongue darted out and he hissed a breath."

Frowning at him with concern, she ran her eyes down his length, "You okay?"

"Yeah, just have a crick in my back, that's all. I was thinking, you said you've never climbed a tree before, right?" Ryker delighted in the wary grimace on her face.

"Uh, right, but—"

"Now's as good a time as any, duchess. Come on, I'll show you how it's done." Grabbing her hand, he dragged her around to the front of the house where the massive maple tree stood. Its long limbs stretching gracefully toward the sky, reaching for the sunshine.

"Ryker, this is not a good idea. I have to get cleaned up before the meeting tonight. I do not have time to go have a broken arm set." Claudia stopped in her tracks, and crossed her arms under her breasts, plumping them up and making his mouth go dry.

He consider dropping it, but then he caught a glimpse of the tiny diamond chip earring glinting in her earlobe, and the two hundred dollar sneakers on her feet that were now dotted with paint spatters. She needed someone to help her expand her horizons, and if he couldn't take her to bed, then he was damn sure going to ingrain himself in her memory banks.

"Chicken."

The one word had exactly the right effect. She bristled, and her eyes flared to life with annoyance at the challenge. "It's not cowardly to avoid putting oneself in harm's way."

A loud bark of laughter burst from his chest, "And that, duchess, is exactly why you're going to haul your cute ass up into the tree one way or another. No one in Stone River, Texas should ever say "oneself". Now, the first thing you have to do is find a good solid handhold. You want to get a good grip, and up you go." Ryker hauled himself up the tree onto the first limb, and then looked back to see her studying him intently. Unable to wipe the grin from his face, he hopped back down to the ground and jerked his head toward the tree, "Your turn."

Her jaw clenched as she approached the wide tree trunk. With a studious look on her face she reached for the handhold he had used and then stopped when she realized it was too high for her. Turning around, she glared at him, "This is stupid."

"No it's not. You're looking for the easy way by trying to copy me, but climbing trees isn't like walking up a set of stairs. You have to work for it. Look for the handhold that suits you."

With a grunt of irritation she spun back around to face the tree, and this time she searched the grooves and hollows of the old bark until she found a grip that worked for her height. In a determined but shaky move, she lifted herself up onto the lowest tree branch, and found a seat. The triumph on her beautiful face sent a wave of pride washing over him.

"Well done. Now, turn and face the trunk again, and look for the next strongest branch. You want to make sure to only use the thickest branches so you don't hurt the tree by breaking off its young limbs."

The tinkle of her giggle reached his ears. "It's not the tree I'm worried about hurting, Ryker." She managed to move up another three or four feet before she turned back to him with a frown. "Get your ass up here, Mr. Tree hugger. I'm not going to be the only one with a broken neck if this goes bad."

Laughing all the way, Ryker quickly made his way up the tree on the opposite side from her. They were nearly level and a good twenty-five feet off the ground when he indicated she should stop and look around. Up this high, the branches were thinner, and the smaller leaves were greener. The view of the yard and the neighborhood was spectacular from this angle.

"I can almost see Main Street from here!" she gasped, her pleasure obvious in the smile on her face.

"If you look this way you can see the St. Andrews Church spire on the other end of town." He pointed out the white peak that was just on the other side of a hill.

The two of them fell into an easy silence as they took in the view from the top. Ryker couldn't remember the last time he'd climbed a tree, but it had never been as much fun as this. Seeing Claudia experience something new made him feel like a better man. He wanted to spend the rest of his life experiencing new things with her. Shock hit him square in the gut as he realized what he was thinking. She was still very much a stranger to him, and yet he was already planning a lifetime with her. He must be losing his mind to lust.

"So, now that we're up here, how exactly do we get back down?" Her words interrupted his musings, and it took him a few seconds to formulate a response.

"Same way, just backwards. You have to be extra careful going down. Find a solid spot for your foot. Trust me, gravity will make sure you get down one way or another, it's up to you to make sure it's in one piece," he explained.

She started to move and then froze in place, "I can't do this."

Ryker laughed, "Sure you can, just move slowly, and carefully."

Her head jerked violently as she began to visibly tremble. "No, I *can't* do this, Ryker. I'm scared."

The sudden fear in her wide hazel eyes tore at his heart, and he cursed, "Okay, easy, love. Stay put and I'll come around to you. Don't worry, I'll get you down."

Moving carefully so he didn't jostle her too much, he made his way back down to a branch that split the distance between them, and then twisted around the tree until he was coming up underneath her.

"I'm right below you, Claudia. This is me, putting my hand on your ankle," he could feel her muscles jump when he lightly gripped the ankle and squeezed. "Good girl. Now, I want you to hold onto the branch that runs next to your right hip, that's it, that will give you a good hold for lowering yourself. You're going to slowly sink down with one foot, and I'm going to direct it to a branch so you can get your bearings, okay?"

Her breathing had increased, and the sharp nod she gave him bespoke her fear, but she did as he instructed, and in a moment she was between him and the tree trunk. Kissing her temple, he murmured words of encouragement, and talked her slowly down the tree. The moment her feet were on the ground, she spun in his arms and hugged him tight pressing her face into his chest.

"Thank God! I thought I was going to fall."

Chuckling, he dropped a kiss to the crown of her head, inhaling the scent of cocoa butter and vanilla mixed with feminine sweat. "I would never let you get hurt."

They stood there for several heartbeats, tightly wrapped together. Ryker's heart ached for things he couldn't have as he took note of every curve of her wickedly formed body pressed against his own. He considered telling her how he felt, but then tossed the thought aside when he pictured Mack's face in his brain. A douchebag he might be, but he would never do anything to hurt Mack or Claudia, and coming between them would hurt them both. It was clear he was stuck between the proverbial rock and a hard place, only the hard place was his groin.

Shifting his hips, he lifted his head, and smiled down at her. "How was it?"

"Before the scary part it was awesome. Thank you for teaching me to climb a tree, Ryker. I'm not sure I would have even tried it without you." As she moved away from him, she looked down at her dirty sweaty clothes and grimaced. "I better clean up before the meeting."

"Definitely, come on, I'll scrub your back." He made like he was going to lead her into the house, and she laughed.

"No you don't, Casanova. I'll scrub my own back thank you very much. Are you coming tonight?"

Winking at her, he nodded, "Definitely. Guess I better go back to my own cold lonely shower."

"If it's cold you're not doing it right. There's this little lever that makes it warm if you just turn it a bit…" she teased, and he swatted her ass playfully as she hurried toward the house.

"Yeah you better run. Do you need a ride tonight?"

She waved from the steps, "Nope, I'm good. I'll see you then, and thanks for—well, for everything today. I had a lot of fun."

"Me too, duchess." He watched as she walked into her house, the screen door shutting silently behind her. It was getting harder and harder to deny his attraction to her, but being cut out of her life completely would be worse.

He knew she had slept with Mack. Good grief the man was happier than a cat in the sun lately. It was obvious he had gotten laid. And it just stung Ryker that much more. The woman making his brother so happy was the same one, he wanted for himself.

CHAPTER EIGHT

After a mind-boggling three-hour showdown with the citizens of Stone River, the Granite Estates project was no more. The town hadn't been interested in Claudia's facts and figures, or the idea of expanding their education system, and population. They were intent on Stone River remaining a small town, and there was nothing she or anyone else at Schmidt Properties could do about it.

Her ego was deflated, her pride was bruised, and her stomach was twisted into knots. Never had she fought so hard to make people believe she was in the right, while questioning her own motives. She believed in her father's company, but she also believed that Stone River was pretty damn perfect the way it was. It turned her arguments to the town on their nose, and she couldn't seem to find the same fire in her soul she felt when she first arrived in town.

It was possible that her father would accept her defeat, but she hated having to ask it of him. This was one of those chance of a lifetime assignments that could have shot her to the top of the company, and assured all of the naysayers that she had the chops to run Schmidt Properties one day. It didn't matter the idea of being CEO left a sour taste in her mouth, because it wasn't nearly as foul tasting as the bitter defeat she had been handed tonight by the tiny population of this town.

When everyone rose to leave the town hall meeting, she remained seated facing the front of the emptying room. She didn't know what else there was to say to anyone. Humiliation burned in her gut. For the first time since she arrived in Stone River she truly felt out of place.

It was several moments before her brain registered the warmth surrounding her was an arm around her shoulders. Turning her head, she met Ryker's gray-blue eyes, surprised to find sympathy but no pity in them. His silent comfort meant more to her than she could have verbalized, so she just relished it, absorbing the warmth he offered with greedy hunger.

He continued to hold her in silence until several new voices echoed through the empty meeting room. Mack's deep baritone tickled something inside of her, but it was Ryker she turned to when he withdrew his arm. Her fingers laced through his, and she gripped his hand between hers, refusing to give up the connection with him yet. For a moment she thought she saw a flash of reverence in his gaze, but he quickly pushed it aside and gave her stoic sympathy again.

As Mack took the seat on her other side, she realized two things. The first was that she was more at home between these two brothers than she had ever been in her life, and she was now firmly caught up in an unusual love triangle she didn't know how to explain. The second was that she wasn't alone.

Rachel Brooks had followed him in, along with another pretty woman with long dark hair and expressive ocean blue eyes. The new woman had the delicate features of a playful fairy, but her body was curvy, and her smile was genuine.

"How ya doing, sweetheart?" Mack asked softly. He reached for her hand, hesitating when he saw her gripping Ryker's between her fists, choosing instead to rest his palm on her upper thigh.

Forcing back the urge to move from between the only two men who had ever made her burn with need, she gave him a tight smile. "I'm fine. This is a big disappointment for Schmidt Properties, but we'll survive."

"Claudia, this is Zoey Keegan." Rachel filled the awkward silence, and the newly introduced Zoey held out a hand forcing Claudia to release her hold on Ryker. She was pleased when he covered her opposite thigh in a mirror image of his brother. *Two hands of support to hold me up*, she thought ruefully.

"Nice to meet you, Mrs. Keegan," she said politely, pulling her business persona back on for the introduction.

Zoey wasn't having it though, and after the handshake she waved off the formalities. "I'm just Zoey, trust me. Mrs. Keegan sounds weird. I still can't even manage to sign a check with the right last name, so there's no reason to use it yet. I wanted to offer my sympathy on the negative vote tonight, but it seems you've got a lot of supporters."

Zoey looked down pointedly at the matching hands on Claudia's lap, but there was no censorship there, just pure feminine knowledge. "The Thompson brothers have been good friends to me since I moved here," she explained, allowing herself to rest her head on Mack's shoulder as the stress from the last several weeks of planning slipped out of her, leaving only exhaustion.

"Of that I have no doubt," Zoey said with a wink. "Rachel and I were thinking after everything tonight you might need a ladies' night, and considering we both live in houses bursting with testosterone, we would like one too."

"Will there be alcohol?" Claudia asked. Relief washed through her as everyone laughed.

Rachel nodded vigorously, "Absolutely! No ladies' night is complete without it."

"Then as long as it can wait until tomorrow, I'm in. Tonight I think I need a glass of wine and a long hot soak in the tub," Claudia said with a heavy sigh.

"It's a date!" Zoey replied, "We'll meet at Robin's tomorrow evening. About eight?"

Claudia smiled back, "Sounds good. See you two then, and thanks for inviting me."

The two women said their goodbyes and left the meeting room. For several moments Claudia remained frozen in time, head on Mack's shoulder, covering their two hands with her own as they rested in her lap. If she didn't count the fact she had just nailed the final coffin in her rise to the CEO position at Schmidt Properties, the moment was blissfully perfect. There was no way her father would give her the reins now. It was odd how little emotional response she felt for the loss. Instead of pain, or regret, she just felt empty.

"I'm sorry, Claudia. I know how much you wanted this project to go through," Mack said sweetly. Ryker remained unusually quiet.

"It's alright. It's part of the business. You win some, you lose some, right?" she replied.

"Do you always handle let down so easily?" he asked with a cynical laugh.

Shaking her head, she sighed, "The problem isn't losing the project. Granite Estates was doomed from the beginning. The guy who started the project thought he could circumvent the town planning board by buying up enough of the property in question. Thanks to his boneheaded move, Schmidt Properties owns a dozen or so homes that will have to be sold at a loss, or turned into rental units."

"So, if he was the one who started this, why did you get sent down here to clean it up?" Mack asked, turning his hand so their palms were mashed together, and linking their fingers.

"My father. He gave me the chance to prove myself by getting this project under control, but now...well I don't know what he'll say." She hated hearing that wistful tone in her own voice. It wasn't her fault the town didn't want to be bought up, so it wasn't worth feeling guilty over.

The more she told herself that, the more her stomach tightened. It might not have been her fault, but it was her job, and a Schmidt always gets the job done. "I need to head for home. That wine is calling my name."

She stood, letting both of their hands fall away from her. Ryker watched her warily, but Mack rose to his feet and brushed a comforting kiss over her lips. "I hitched a ride with Rogan and Rachel, or I would offer to take you home." Suddenly he jerked his eyes to his brother. Claudia saw him swallow hard and clench his jaw just before he addressed Ryker. "Would you mind making sure she gets home okay, since you brought your car?"

Ryker looked just as surprised at the request as Claudia. "Of course I will, but it's okay if you want to take my car. I can catch a ride back with the Brooks family."

Mack shook his head, "No, unfortunately I still have a few chores to do at the ranch before I can head to the cabin. I would appreciate it if you would take her and make sure she's settled."

~ ~ ~

Already kicking himself for the dumbass move, Mack continued to run his mouth virtually handing Claudia over to Ryker on a silver platter. His heart was torn in two by the idea she could still choose his younger brother over him, but after the last week he knew he had to take the chance and trust her. It was too late to question the decision anyway.

"I brought my car, gentleman. I'll be just fine," Claudia said. Her voice was stern and the warmth in her eyes had hardened into gold chips of regret. She was physically pulling away from him, but in his heart he knew she needed comforting.

"I don't mind, duchess. It's not like I have anything better to do," Ryker said with forced casualness. His questioning look was too much for Mack right now.

"It would make me feel better, sweetheart. I just want to make sure you get home and tucked in safely." Mack wrapped his hand around the nape of her neck to remind her who was in control of the moment. Just that simple act of dominance seemed to ease the stress lines ringing her eyes, and her eyelids flickered.

Shrugging her shoulders, she pulled on arrogance like a fine coat, and snapped out, "Stone River is probably the safest place on the map, but fine, follow me if you must."

When she would have stormed away from him, Mack spun her around and gripped her by the chin. "Easy, Claudia. I know you're not used to anyone caring what happens to you, but you better work on getting more comfortable with it. Ryker will take care of you in my stead, and in doing so he allows me to go back to the ranch and finish the business I need to handle without worrying. You're important to me, so let me coddle you a bit."

The surprise in her eyes made his dick hard. This was the first time he had really pulled out the Dom card and thrown it on the table. His voice was hard, but calm, and his grip was firm without bruising her. With just the gesture she knew he meant business, but his words let her accept submission easier.

Dropping another kiss on her parted lips, he whispered goodbye and then nodded at Ryker before hurrying to catch up with the Brooks'. Somewhere inside he knew leaving Claudia alone with Ryker would come back to bite him, but he couldn't avoid it forever, and ultimately if he was what she needed to convince her to stay in Stone River then Mack would step aside. He just prayed it didn't come to that.

~ ~ ~

Ryker watched Claudia, as she watched Mack walk out of the meeting room. Her eyes were hooded with desire, but their light was dimmer than before. Something inside of her seemed to break when the vote was announced, and Ryker felt an odd need to fix it for her.

Her pretty blonde hair was pulled up into a tight twist at the back of her head, and she wore a severe looking suit, with heels that brought her lips about four inches closer to his mouth. Gold jewelry glinted in the fluorescent lighting, giving her an aura of elegance. The woman before him was not the same one who scraped the paint off her own house two days ago in cutoff shorts. This woman was poised, and refined. She oozed class, and old school money. She was exactly the type of woman he had avoided throughout his ten-year football career, because she was a man-eater. The type of woman who could put a man in his place, lead a board meeting, and order drapes for her home simultaneously and without breaking a sweat. And God help him, she made him harder than a cement wall.

For the last week he had thought of almost nothing but her. He imagined stripping her clothes off so he could touch and taste every curve of her body. The desire just to be close to her kept him lying in his bed awake stroking his cock and finding no satisfaction. If she had this much control over him after such a short time, what would it be like if she stayed here permanently, and worse, if she chose Mack.

"Are you done yet?" the angry tone of her voice brought his eyes back up to hers, and he lifted his eyebrow at her question. "Are you done undressing me with your eyes? I'm really rather exhausted, and if this is how you honor your brother's request then he's not going to be particularly happy with you."

"Down, duchess. Just because I'm admiring the packaging, doesn't mean I'm going to tear the paper off. This whole evening has got you pretty rattled, huh?" he cocked his head as he watched sadness flash in her eyes.

"Not at all. Like I said, this is just the way it happens sometimes. I'm sure there is already a new project waiting for me in Austin."

She collected the papers she had used in her presentation, piling them neatly and then sliding them into her laptop bag. The efficient bravado was like a dare to him. He wanted to see the fire in her eyes again. The desire, which boiled his blood and made him ache.

Instead, he held out his hand silently for her to take. He honestly didn't think she would accept it, but pleasure coursed through him when she did so after only a brief hesitation. She might argue it, but on some level she wanted him.

~ ~ ~

Claudia let Ryker lead her out of the meeting hall, only to find it was pouring rain outside when they reached the door. "Hang on. Where are your keys, love?" he asked, bringing her to a standstill when she would have pushed through the glass door into the rain.

She dug in her purse for her keys, and before she could protest he gallantly took them from her and darted out into the rain leaving her gaping after him. He brought her sexy Benz up to the front door as efficiently as her father's personal valet might have, and then held the door open as she slid into the leather driver's seat.

"I'll be right behind you, duchess," he said softly, before the door shut with a click, and he ran for his own car.

A shiver of desire went through her, and she couldn't peel her eyes away from his denim covered ass. Even through the blurry wet window she could see the tight muscles bunching and releasing as he moved. God, he was beautiful, so like Mack, and yet so different. The two men were like the two antique bookends she had on her desk at home. Separate they were lovely, but together they were magnificent.

Dragging her attention back to the wheel, she made the drive home. Janet Jackson pumped through the stereo, singing about making love in the rain. The irony of those words wasn't lost on her, and she snickered at how much it matched the unusual mood she was in. Her body ached to be held close and comforted, but her mind was rejecting the need for soothing. As a well-grounded, independent woman she shouldn't need anyone to pat her on the back and reassure her she had done a good job in the light of her defeat. She also knew if she let Ryker get his hands on her, there was no way she was going to be able to stop it at a comforting snuggle—and it scared the hell out of her. She couldn't do that to Mack. It wouldn't be right.

Parking in her driveway, she felt a pang of regret as she remembered she would likely have to sell the pretty piece of property. It wasn't like she needed a home in Stone River when she would be living and working in Austin. Even if it was exactly what she wanted to do.

Ryker met her at the front door, and again he took her keys from her to open the door. She frowned at him as he followed her into the living room. "I didn't realize following me home included both valet and concierge services. Is there a turn down service as well?"

When his eyes snapped to hers, her whole mouth dried up. Fire lit their grayish-blue depths, and arrogance curved his lips up into a small smirk. "I can provide all kinds of services if you're in need, sweet cheeks. Just give me the word."

They were both holding their breath. She could see it in the tense lines of his big body, and feel it in her own chest. It was unspoken desire. A thirst for each other's bodies that was really becoming unbearable.

"Claudia, I know you want me as much as I want you," he said softly, stroking the back of his knuckle down her cheek.

Stiffening her spine, she nodded, "You're right. I do want you, but I want Mack too, so how do you suppose it's going to work? Do you plan on a ménage relationship with me, or are you two going to just pass me back and forth like a shared toy?"

He let out a hiss of irritation and took a step backward. Shoving his hand into his wet hair, and growling in frustration, "I don't share well."

"Yeah, I got that impression, so I guess we're back to square one. As friends," she said, putting her laptop bag down on the dining room table and releasing her hair from the tight twist at the nape of her neck. With the water in it, it was barely hanging on, the sudden relief to the muscles in her neck nearly made her weep with joy.

Before she could turn around, Ryker was behind her, pinning her against the table, with his hands tangled in her long locks, nails scratching at her scalp. His hot breath scorched the back of her ear as he spoke into it, "Friends isn't going to work, Claudia, because I don't have a fucking hard-on for my friends. I don't lay awake at night wondering what my friend's pussy tastes like, and what it would feel like to sink into her heat. So you can understand why I don't think I can be friends with you."

"Oh my God," she moaned, trying desperately to grasp the lost tendrils of control she had been holding all evening.

"That's right, duchess. I want you naked and spread on my bed waiting for me, begging for the pleasure only I can give you," he hissed, nipping the soft lobe of her ear, and grinding his hard erection against her ass cheeks.

His words were so similar to Mack's it froze her blood in her veins and she surged upward, shoving him backward and moving to the other side of the table before he could react. "Stop it. Right now. It's not fair for you to make me choose, damn it. I didn't come here to meet men. I came here to do my fucking job, and now my job is over. Clearly I need to get my shit together and go home before I lose myself into these mind games you and your brother are playing with me."

"You would run away just because you want both of us?" He looked stunned and slightly deflated.

"I have to go home, Ryker. My job is in Austin."

Staring at each other across the table, panting for air, and struggling with feelings neither one wanted to feel, Claudia could feel every cell in her body calling out to his, aching for him to climb over the imaginary divide and force her to accept the truth. She wasn't going to leave Stone River with her heart intact. It was already too late for that.

"Well I guess you just put me in my place, didn't you, duchess. Enjoy your wine and your bath. I'll let Mack know you got home safe and sound." He spun on his heel and disappeared out the front door without another word.

The moment the front door slammed shut, Claudia's knees buckled and she collapsed into a chair. Her entire body was violently trembling as she fought back the wave of emotion that hit her. Regret, sadness, defeat, and loss all burned in her brain and in her heart. She had never felt so exposed and vulnerable as she did here in this tiny town. It was time to go home.

Pulling her cell phone from her purse, she hit the speed dial for the only person she ever shared her secrets with, and held her breath. When her mother's voice came on the line, all of the tears she had been holding back burst free.

"Claudy? What's wrong, honey? Did something happen?"

"I messed up, Mom. The project fell through," she hiccuped into the phone.

Linda Schmidt was quiet for a moment, before asking, "Please tell me that you are not crying over a stupid business deal."

"Mom, this was a really big deal, dad said—"

"Your dad says a lot of things, but you know his bark is worse than his bite. Are you really this worked up over a lost project, or is something else going on?" Leave it to her mother to nail the heart of the hurt.

"I think I fell in love."

The sharp inhale on the other end of the line wasn't encouraging. "I guess I'm still confused, Claudy. Falling in love is something to be happy about, right?"

"If I tell you this, will you promise not to tell daddy?"

"What did you do?"

"Promise?"

"Fine, I promise. What is going on?"

"There are these two cowboys—"

"Two?" The shock in her mother's voice made Claudia hesitate. Maybe telling her was a bad idea. "Claudia? Are you there?"

"I'm here. Yes, two. They are brothers, and in this strange little town it seems to be the norm for brothers to hook up with the same girl," she explained, listening to the sharp inhale of her mother's breath as she absorbed that bit before continuing, "but these two brothers don't seem to want a ménage relationship. They both want to be with me, but they don't want to be with me together. And I'm afraid I've fallen in love with both of them. I don't know how to choose, or what to do, and now I'm going back to Austin to face dad—"

"Stop making your dad out to be some sort of demon. He loves you, Claudy. He isn't going to skin you alive over anything."

"Even if I end up in a relationship with two men?"

This time Linda's hesitation was even more obvious, "I'll be honest, it's a shock, and it's not going to be easy to accept. How does that even work? You can't marry two different people, so why would you want to build a life with them?"

"Because I can't pick which one of them that I could give up. They've gotten under my skin, and they are in my bones now, Mom. If they weren't so against a permanent ménage I would try it."

"Maybe you should listen to their reasons for not wanting this, Claudy. Think about how you would be ostracized for the family you have? Your children would have to grow up with two fathers in one home, and kids are mean these days. We sheltered you so much from reality by schooling you privately, but you have to understand that some things just aren't done."

"They are here, Mom. There are at least two other families with multiple partners."

Linda sighed, "Oh, sweetie, you're in a small town, not Austin. Just because that small number of people accept alternative lifestyles doesn't mean the rest of the world will."

"So I should walk away from them?"

"I didn't say that. The only thing I'm worried about is your happiness. Keeping you safe and happy is all I've ever cared about, and believe it or not, that goes for your father too. He may be a hard-ass in business, and I know he wasn't always there—" Linda's voice cracked on the other end of the line, and Claudia felt her tears come harder, "but he did his best. If those two men love you enough to do their best for you, then I will support any relationship that keeps you happy."

Relief poured through Claudia's body, and she felt all of her muscles relaxing. "Thank you, Mom. I needed to know that. I think I'll come home this weekend to clear things up at work. I'll need time to plan for a new project, and sell my house here in Stone River if dad transfers me."

"First you need to tell him about the men you're seeing, Claudy. I'm sure he'll let you stay in Stone River if that's where you want to be."

That was the problem. Claudia wasn't really sure where she wanted to be. Between her feelings for Mack, and her unavoidable addiction to Ryker, she felt torn in two, but she did feel at home here in Stone River. Maybe just staying put for now was smart, at least until she figured out what she wanted out of her relationship with the Thompson brothers.

"I'll talk to him this weekend. Thanks, Mom, I've missed talking to you."

Linda laughed, "My phone number hasn't changed, young lady. All you have to do is dial."

"I promise I'll do it more often. Love you, Mom."

"I love you too, Claudy. See you this weekend."

As the phone clicked off in her ear, Claudia finally stopped crying. Her mother was right. There was nothing more important than happiness. Sure there were hardships involved with a ménage, but there was no way she was going to be able to give up either brother, so she needed to bring them around to her way of thinking. If they couldn't get with the program, then she was better off moving back to Austin.

~ ~ ~

Ryker slammed into the cabin feeling hopeless, helpless, and horny. The only woman in more than a decade to make his dick impossibly hard and she wasn't willing to give him a chance if he wouldn't share her with his older brother. How much more fucked up could his life get?

Mack was standing in the kitchen in the dark, drinking one of his beers, and Ryker lashed out at him. "I thought you had shit to do at the ranch? Isn't your boss going to be pissed you cut out early? Oh wait, that's right, you have a whole fucking family of bosses. If you don't like what one says, you can just ask another."

Instead of punching him, Mack cocked his head and gave him a half smile. "So she didn't let you seduce her?"

Ryker froze in his tracks. Staring back at his brother, he suddenly felt like a royal ass. "I seem to have a knack for being a dick. I'm sorry. And no, she didn't let me seduce her. She won't because she wants you too. *Fuck*! What kind of a mess are we involved in with her, Mack?"

Sighing heavily, Mack opened the fridge and retrieved two fresh beers, passing him one before he led the way into the living room. Ryker took his chair, while Mack sprawled on the couch and propped his booted foot up on the coffee table.

"You know this is the first time in nearly a year you have had something besides your former career to bitch about."

Ryker choked on his beer, and sputtered for an answer. "I guess she's a good distraction."

"Damn right she is. The way I see it, she is too caught up in what's wrong or right for you and me. Or maybe we're the ones who aren't prioritizing right." Mack's thoughtful look and odd choice of words left Ryker scratching at his beard in confusion.

"Spit it out, asshole. What are you trying to say?" he snapped at his older brother.

Mack shrugged, "I want her happy. I'll do whatever it takes to keep her here and make her happy. What about you?"

His shock level had never been higher in his life, and he couldn't formulate words to respond. When he rolled out of surgery and the doctor told him his career was over, he had felt a genuine physical loss in his life. It still burned in his soul. Then when the bank contacted him about his bouncing checks, and the funds management company his accountant worked for admitted all of his money had been transferred to an offshore account, he had been pissed. Shocked, but pissed. None of that compared to his astonishment over Mack's question. He was offering to share his woman with Ryker, and at this moment Ryker wasn't sure he could say the same.

"I don't know if she would ever accept me the way she's accepted you. She slept with you," Ryker said, staring down at his hands.

"How do you know?" Mack asked.

Rolling his eyes, Ryker glared at him, "You came home strutting like a bull in mating season, brother. Don't try to deny it."

"Wouldn't dream of it," Mack said, shaking his head. "But I think you and I better figure out where we stand, because she's on the verge of running, Ryk, and I don't know if I'll survive it. Losing my business brought me to a low place, but losing my woman and my brother in one blow would kill me."

"You aren't losing me, Mack. And besides, you could rebuild the business if you wanted to. Hell, I'll help you. We can take some of my money from selling the house and we'll buy one of those properties Schmidt's going to be dumping cheap. We'll turn it into a workshop, and you can create while I sell."

"You know, it's not a half bad idea," Mack said, before shaking his head. "I'm not good in business though, Ryk, and it would be a hell of a risk. I also know you don't want to be tied to Stone River forever."

Ryker stared back at his brother in confusion, "It's not Stone River that's the problem, it's the lack of direction. If I had a reason to stay..."

His words drifted off, and he watched Mack absorb them in thoughtful silence. They both drank their beers as they mulled over the possibilities in front of them. Mack was absolutely right, there were a lot of risks involved with rebuilding the leather working business, but Ryker wanted to do this for his brother. If nothing else, it was a way to repay him for his kindness in the last year. Mack had put up with a lot of shit no one else would, and Ryker owed him.

"We could make it work, Mack. You have way too much talent to be working horses and mucking stalls for the rest of your life."

Mack frowned back at him, "I don't even know if I could sell a saddle anymore. People have forgotten my name by now. It was different when everyone in Texas knew who I was."

"Let me do some research at least. If we can't sell saddles here in po-dunk Stone River, Texas, home of the cowboy, then maybe you're right about it being a bad investment," Ryker agreed, holding his breath. Until this very moment he hadn't realized how much he desperately wanted his older brother's approval again.

Growing up, he and Mack had had an ideal childhood. They were the best of friends until high school when Ryker began taking football more seriously. By the time Ryker graduated, Mack had already left home and was apprenticing for another leather artist. It wasn't the same tight knit relationship as before, but they still talked regularly. As the years passed, they drifted further apart, and before long, the only time they spoke was at Thanksgiving and Christmas. When their father died, Ryker had only been able to fly in for a two-day visit for the funeral because of his schedule. He had left Mack holding the reins of the family, even though he knew Mack was dealing with his business going bankrupt.

Since then their mother had deteriorated into Alzheimer's and Mack was the one who made the effort to drive to Dallas once a month to see her. Each time Ryker made some excuse to skip the trip, because he wasn't ready to face a stranger who didn't recognize him. How many other ways had Mack taken control and handled things for him, so he could continue being selfish and immature? A deep sense of regret and acceptance filled his chest, as he realized just how much his older brother had sacrificed for him. Perhaps it was time to return the favor.

"If she chooses you I'll back off," Ryker said, feeling the sting of the words straight through to the bone. "I just want her happy."

The wide smile on Mack's face was slightly unsettling. "That's what I was hoping you would say, little brother. I have a plan, and it involves you pulling out all of your best moves and seducing her. Are you in?"

Ryker hesitated, shocked by Mack's reaction. He had expected him to say thanks and leave it at that. The fact that he wanted Ryker to stay involved was mindboggling. Leaning forward, tense with anticipation, he listened as Mack began to fill him in on how they could work together to reroute Claudia's plan for her future.

CHAPTER NINE

"Thank you for inviting me out tonight, ladies. You have no idea how much I needed this." Claudia accepted her seven and seven from the bartender, and followed Rachel and Zoey across the half empty bar to a table.

"I'm just glad you joined us. Rach and I really only have each other to hang out with, and I can only take so much of this wench. You'll understand when you know her better," Zoey said, winking conspiratorially.

Rachel smacked her shoulder, "Hey! I resent that."

"You mean you resemble that?" Zoey asked, waving to get the waitress's attention. "So what are we eating, ladies? Salads or cheese fries?"

Claudia and Rachel both answered together, "Cheese fries," and then burst into laughter.

"Thank God you're not one of those prissy women who pretends not to eat real food," Rachel said. "Lately it seems all of my new clients are city folks who want to buy a country home. It's painful to take them to lunch. If I wanted to watch a rabbit eat grass I could sit on my back patio."

Nodding in understand, Claudia wrinkled her nose, "I have to do my share of grass eating when I'm back home, trust me. Here I feel like I can relax and enjoy myself. Nobody seems to care if I'm thirty pounds overweight."

Zoey looked askance at her, "Overweight? You're joking right?" She flashed an irritated look at Rachel, "She's got to be joking, right?"

"I don't think so, Z. Sounds pretty serious. I think she's been poisoned by the city. It's all the carbon monoxide and crowded spaces. Just does things to the brain." Rachel was shaking her head in resignation. "It will take us years to undo the brainwashing."

"You two are hysterical. I've always fought my weight, but lately I haven't fought as hard. There's something ridiculously comforting about a giant cheeseburger with bacon on it." Claudia sighed wistfully and sipped her drink.

"Years, I tell ya," Rachel whispered to Zoey. They both wore matching sad expressions, making Claudia giggle and roll her eyes.

"So please tell me how you two ladies managed to snag almost a whole baseball team of sexy Texas men between you?" she asked, propping her chin up on her hand and finding a comfortable seat for the story. "Your families are the only families like this I've ever met, and I'm curious how it happened."

Rachel smiled, "I started the whole ball of wax. Actually my guys did. See, I had been dating a guy named Mitch who cheated on me—"

"Douchebag," Zoey grumbled under her breath, making Claudia laugh.

"An enormous one! Anyway, when the four guys—Rogan, Parker, Sawyer, and Hudson—found out I was single they decided to make a play for me. I opened the door by seeking out a one-night stand—"

Zoey interrupted again, "You mean you kicked the door open and waved your perky tits at them!"

"I did no such thing!" Rachel said indignantly.

"You came to Robin's that night planning to have a rowdy romp with a random cowboy. If that's not offering up a buffet to a starving crowd then I don't know what is," Zoey said.

Their waitress brought their cheese fries and they all dug in. Claudia grinned as she watched the other two women enjoy the fattening treat. It was nice to be out with females who weren't looking at her like competition. Once they had all eaten enough to stave off starvation, she prodded for more of the story.

"So you came to the bar looking to get laid, and then what?" she asked.

"Before I could even put my plan into action the Brooks brothers spotted me and they offered up their...er...services for the weekend," Rachel said, blushing slightly.

"The weekend?" Claudia lifted an eyebrow at the pretty brunette.

"The *whole* weekend. Nothing but hot monkey sex with four hunks for a whole weekend. Can you believe it?" Zoey said, throwing her hands up in the air. "Lucky bitch."

"The agreement was I would spend the weekend with them at their ranch and then we would walk away friends. No strings attached," Rachel finished.

Reaching out, Claudia took Rachel's hand and stared pointedly at the enormous diamond adorning her left ring finger. "Looks like we need to have a discussion about what "no strings attached" means, hon."

Zoey let out a bark of laughter and Rachel's blush deepened. "Well I did walk away against my better judgment, but what I didn't know when I left their house that day was they had already sealed the deal. I found out a couple of months later I was pregnant with Juliet, and when I told them, it changed everything. We've had our ups and downs though, don't get me wrong. How many relationships are rock-solid after only forty-eight hours of wild sex? They didn't even have to live through PMS for the first nine months of our relationship."

"I think Sawyer nearly cracked the first time you got your period. He showed up at the ranch begging Tanner to hide him," Zoey snorted.

"Wow. I can't even imagine what went through your head when you realized they wanted you to be in a permanent relationship with all four of them. Do you know whose baby it is?" Claudia asked.

Rachel shook her head, "It never mattered. From the moment she was conceived Juliet had four fathers who loved her. We're very lucky ladies her and I."

"How did the town react?" Claudia asked and then she cringed, "I'm sorry, I'm being very rude with my nosey questions."

Shrugging, Rachel smiled, "Don't worry about it. I've been asked much worse, and we're friends. Or at least I hope you consider us friends." After Claudia nodded her agreement, she continued, "The town was shocked of course, and there have been a handful of negative reactions, but for the most part they are supportive. I grew up here and the Brooks family is one of the founding families of Stone River. They can pretty much do whatever they want around here."

"It's the same with my guys. The Keegan family didn't help found the town, but they've been here for several generations. They have donated so much money to the school system and the town I think Tanner could walk through it just wearing a hat and spurs and not get even a raised eyebrow," Zoey said.

Claudia sipped at her drink while silently wondering how she might have reacted if one of her coworkers showed up at work and made the announcement she was marrying four brothers. It would certainly ruffle feathers back home. Her father's most of all. He would go apeshit if he knew she was even flirting with both of the Thompson brothers.

"How did the guys know sharing a woman was what they wanted?" she asked.

Zoey snorted, "Mine didn't exactly. I've always had a thing for Tanner, but the one time I reached out to him he was a jerk, so I forced myself to give up on the possibility of us getting together. When my apartment got bought out by Schmidt last summer I had to find a new place to live. Thanks to my mom I barely had two plug nickels in my pocket, and Tanner was the only person I knew I could stay with until I found a place."

"Wow. So you became his roommate and then just fell in love with him and his brothers?" Claudia asked.

"Of course not. His two brothers, Dalton and Clint, were smarter than Tanner was. They fell in love with me first, and the three of us had to work to convince him it was in his best interest. It's hard to believe we've been married for almost six months already," Zoey said, twisting the platinum wedding ring on her finger.

"You're telling me! We're getting ready to celebrate our two year anniversary!" Rachel exclaimed. "As hard as juggling four husbands is, I wouldn't go back for all the money in the world. Those guys and our baby girl are my happily ever after."

Claudia dropped back against the back of her chair with a huff. "I want a happily ever after."

The other two women exchanged a glance and she would swear they shared a wicked glint in their eyes when they turned back to her. Zoey took the first shot, "So what's between you and the Thompson boys?"

Shrugging, she frowned at the question, "I wish I knew. I met Mack first, and there was just something about him. A spark between us like I've never experienced before. Then when I walked into the bar the other night and met Ryker, it was like an electric shock. When I'm with only one of them I feel happy, but when I'm with the two of them I feel sublime."

"Sounds like Stone River's newest inductees to the polyamorous lifestyle to me," Rachel said, smiling cockily.

"Not likely," Claudia said with a snort. "The two of them are not interested in trying ménage. At least not on a permanent basis. And I'm going back to Austin soon to get my marching orders."

Zoey's eyes widened, "Excuse me? Going back?"

Nodding, Claudia felt the heavy pull of depression in her heart. She didn't want to leave Stone River, but by staying she was just delaying the inevitable. It was important she talk to her father and explain what happened with the Granite Estates project. Perhaps there was still a solution to be found so the whole project wasn't scrapped.

"Well if you're taking the easy way out, we had better take this opportunity to party with you while we can!" Rachel said, jumping to her feet and downing the last of her drink. "Let's go, ladies. This bar needs a bit of livening up." With that, the bubbly brunette seemed to let her fashionable real estate persona slip even further into the background as she took the dance floor. As the lone occupant of the thirty square foot space, Rachel rocked her hips in time to Josh Turner's deep baritone singing, "Firecracker."

"We better join her, so she doesn't get herself arrested," Zoey said, grabbing Claudia's hand and leading her out to the floor.

The three women rocked and bopped to the music for several songs. After the first couple of minutes as the only dancers, they found themselves joined by several other ladies, and a few gentlemen. Quickly the quiet somber crowd filling the bar on a weekday evening began enjoying the spark of excitement.

Claudia couldn't remember when she had enjoyed herself more. Good friends, good food, good music, and the freedom to dance. It was heaven. The only thing missing was the two men who seemed to dominate her thoughts lately.

As much as she liked the idea of finding a happy ending with two gorgeous, sweet men like Mack and Ryk, she knew the logistics were more complicated. It wasn't realistic to believe otherwise, and she was nothing if pragmatic. In a couple of days, she would pack a bag and head for Austin. She needed to find out what was next on her schedule. By now her father would have received her email detailing the decision made by the town, and Gaven Schmidt was known for pulling the trigger quickly. He would already have a Plan B, and possibly a Plan C. She just needed to find out what it was and embrace it. Maybe then she would be able to let go of the hopelessly happy woman she found in Stone River.

~ ~ ~

Ryker was waiting outside the bar when the three women spilled out into the night. They were laughing with a girly abandon that brought a wide smile to his face. Stepping out of the shadows and into the yellow light of the parking lot, he waited for Claudia to notice him.

"Shit. Did I miss curfew again?" she asked. Her tone was half playful and half irritated, with just a hint of tipsy sass.

Zoey snorted, "Uh oh! He's going to crack the whip now."

Rachel sputtered between giggles, "Make him frisk you first! Get the full body cavity search!"

All three women were a laughing heap of bawdy innuendos that might have made Ryker blush if he hadn't spent more than a decade in a locker room. "Alright, ladies, enough. Zoey, Dalton should be here any minute to get you and Rachel. Parker called me and asked me to swing by and check on you when you didn't come home by eleven like you promised."

That sobered Rachel up, and she dug in her purse for her phone, "Shit! I can't believe I'm late! Jules is going to hate me forever!"

"I highly doubt it, Rach. Hell, she just now learned your name was mama," Zoey said, dissolving into girly laughter again at her own joke.

"How much have you been drinking, kitten?" A new voice echoed across the parking lot, and Ryker turned to greet Dalton Keegan as he reached his wife's side.

"Only two, I think. We are drunk on life, and my abs hurt like hell from laughing. You should see Claudia dance! Damn, the girl can shake it like a polaroid picture!" Zoey's antics brought another round of laughter. The atmosphere was so relaxed Ryker found himself chuckling along with the group.

He knew about Claudia's dance skills, he'd seen them himself, but what he hadn't seen was this carefree relaxed goddess, who laughed with her friends, and smiled like the world was at her feet. She looked stunning even with her hair tousled from dancing all night, and her mascara smeared where she wiped away tears of mirth.

Dalton smiled at Ryker, and nodded to Claudia, "You got that one?"

"We're good," he responded, waving the three on as he stood shoulder to shoulder with Claudia. He breathed in her scent, letting the warm cocoa butter flavor of the air around her rest on his taste buds and fill his head. For the rest of his life he would associate cocoa butter with this curvy bombshell.

"Bye, ladies! Thank you for taking me out tonight!" Claudia called out, blowing an energetic kiss to Zoey, who caught it dramatically and then dissolved into giggles again.

Ryker could hear Dalton firmly instructing his wife and her best friend to get into his truck and buckle up, before he turned to face Claudia. Her gorgeous hazel eyes were a warm amber color, and they swallowed him whole the moment he made eye contact.

"So you're playing knight in shining armor tonight again, huh?" she cocked her hip to the side and looked him up and down like a piece of meat. "Does that mean you have to carry me home on your noble steed? Because I'm still really tender from Sunday's ride—"

He snorted, and she blushed lightly as she picked up on the double entendre of her words. "Duchess, I wouldn't be the right cowboy for the whole riding off into the sunset gig. However, since you've been drinking I will be taking you home. We'll get your car tomorrow."

"You know, you're kind of hot when you're being all bossy and serious." She walked toward his car without a backward glance, and he hurried to catch up.

"Thank you. You're kind of hot all the time. I didn't think your ass could look better until I saw it in those jeans. I'll have to write a thank you letter to the manufacturer." He held the car door open for her and smiled when she slid gracefully into the seat. His car was far from a Benz, but she rode in it as though it was gold plated.

"That's the sweetest thing anyone has ever said to me," she said with an astonished look on her face. "I'm not even sure what to say."

He gave her a wink and shut the door so he could walk around and get in himself. "Buckle up, buttercup, no breaking the law in my car."

She rolled her eyes but snapped the seatbelt in place. "Are you going to place your hands at ten and two as well, or is it only certain laws you won't break?"

"Oh no, I'm an excellent driver, and I obey almost all driving laws."

"Last I checked, drunk driving was—"

"Okay!" he interrupted. "Almost all driving laws. Actually, my biggest weakness is speed limits. I used to drive an amateur drag car when I was off season just for kicks." Out of the corner of his eye he saw her mouth drop open. "What? You didn't think my whole life was football did you?"

After a pause, she nodded, "Yeah, I guess I did. What other secret hobbies do you have?"

He smiled at her newfound curiosity, and shrugged, "Not many. I like to play basketball, and golf, and occasionally dress in drag on the weekends. The normal manly hobbies."

Claudia's eyes couldn't get any wider as she gasped in shock, "What?"

"I'm kidding, lighten up! I like guy stuff. Sports, fast cars, pretty girls. I don't cook much, but I'm a grill master. What about you?"

Dropping her head back on the headrest, she relaxed a little and let out a sigh, "I had so many hobbies as a kid I never had much time to slow down. Now as an adult I work all the time, and still don't get a lot of down time. When I do I like to work with my hands. I love refurbishing old worn out things and giving them new life."

"Why didn't you speak up and tell your parents you didn't want to do all of those activities?" Ryker asked. He just couldn't wrap his brain around it, because his life was so carefree as a kid. What would it have been like to be faced with a regimented schedule every day and never have time to be free?

"It just wasn't an option. My parents loved me enough to want me to have every possible opportunity. Perhaps they should have given me more free time, but then I wouldn't be the woman I am today if they had, so I'm grateful for what they did for me. It wasn't always easy, and as a kid I resented all of the schedules and practices, but now I see how it helped me be a stronger businesswoman."

Just like that she turned his first opinion on its top. She was absolutely right. If her parents hadn't pushed her to be so responsible, perhaps life wouldn't have brought her here to Stone River, so he wouldn't wish it any different.

When they arrived at her home, he felt butterflies fill his stomach. This was the moment. He and Mack had agreed he would give the seduction thing one more try. If she was into it, then they would approach her about trying a ménage relationship. If she wasn't, Ryker would walk away for the good of his relationship with his brother.

Taking her keys, he unlocked the door and held it open for her. She dropped her purse on the dining room table and turned back to face him. "Thank you for the ride home, again."

He bowed as elegantly as possible, and gave her a grin, "Always at your service, m'lady. Now, about your payment for services rendered..."

She cocked her hip and her eyebrow rose indignantly, "Payment? You're joking right?"

Shaking his head, he stepped closer, stealing her personal space. "Nope. I think you owe me for dropping everything to ride to the rescue."

"Dropping what? Your evening television and beer routine? And what rescue? I didn't need rescuing thank you very much. I could have gotten a ride home with Zoey and her husband." Her hands were on her hips now and her hazel eyes were flashing fire.

"Mmm, but I think you'll enjoy this payment as much as I do, duchess, so go with it."

Sliding his arms through the openings under hers, he wrapped them around her waist, quickly dragging her up against his body. Before she could protest, he dropped his mouth to hers and kissed her with every ounce of pent up lust that had been raging in his balls for the last week. It rushed through him like a violent summer thunderstorm wreaking havoc on the countryside. The winds of desire laid waste to any protest she might have put up, and before he knew it her hands were clutching at him, holding him closer and riding the swell.

There was nothing gentle about the way he pushed his tongue into her mouth and tasted her. There was no romance, or sweetness in his hands when he cupped her ass, and ground his cock into her soft belly. Only raw lust, and an intriguing need for her to touch him too. Forcing himself to release her lips, he reached up and tugged at her long blonde locks as she stared back at him with glazed eyes heavy with her own need.

Swallowing a groan of lust, he forced his tongue to work in his mouth. "Say yes. Claudia, I need to be inside of you, so say yes. Or better yet, don't say anything at all."

His need had finally overwhelmed her resolve, and suddenly desire dominated both of their motions. Her hands were clawing at his clothes, while her mouth was kissing, nipping, and licking at the skin as it was revealed. She was like a wildcat in his arms, and his cock throbbed in his jeans. Stretching the denim past its comfort zone, and making his brain spin.

Pushing her shirt up to her armpits, he finally got a glimpse of the creamy globes he had been fantasizing about. Vanilla colored and cocoa butter scented, they screamed out to him behind pale pink lace. Mouth watering, he ran his tongue over them at the edge of the fabric. Like magic the skin swelled and rose to meet his teasing mouth. A gentle bite to the dark shadowed curve between them left an indent that brought out some primal satisfaction. He had claimed her as his own. It didn't matter that his brother had traversed her planes and valleys first. All that mattered was she was hot and wet beneath him now.

Flicking open the hook at her back, he peeled back the cups of her bra to find perfect pink nipples reaching out for him. Sucking one between his lips, he added just enough pressure to make her knees wobble beneath her. Sensing his opening, he lifted her into his arms and carried her the short distance to the couch. She went willingly, tugging her shirt the rest of the way off so she was bare now from the waist up. Reaching up, she ran her hands over his naked torso, before lifting her chest to scrape her nipples against his pecks. Fire raced through his loins at the contact, and he hissed out a breath.

"You're going to kill me, duchess."

"If you leave me hanging I'll kill *you*, Ryker."

"Not a chance, love."

He released the button on her jeans and shoved them down to her ankles only to find his process hampered by her shoes. Growling in irritation as she toed the offending canvas off, he hurried to get her completely naked. Once she was divested of every scrap of fabric, he pushed her knees open and sat back on his haunches to stare at the damp curls between her thighs. The fragrance of hot female was heightening his need, and he pressed a kiss to the inside of her knee before placing it on his shoulder.

"Hey wait!" Her hands reached out to still his forward progress and she frowned down at him, "You're not naked yet!"

"If I take my jeans off right now, I'll come all over the carpet, Claudia. Now just lie back and let me taste you."

The smile on her beautiful face was one of pure female satisfaction. *So she liked the thought of him riding the edge, huh? Good to know.* Filing away the new knowledge, he dropped a kiss to the soft curve of her tummy, aware most women were self-conscious about having a curvy belly. He hadn't gotten around to asking her how she felt in particular, but he wanted her to have no doubt he loved every sexy inch of her body.

Using his thumb and forefinger to spread her pussy lips open and up, he inhaled her hot scent deep into his lungs, branding it into his brain forever, and then danced his tongue lightly over her juicy folds. She squealed and wriggled upwards away from him just a bit, but he didn't let it stop his forward progress. Instead he wrapped his unoccupied arm around her thigh to hold her still and went back for seconds of the delicious treat before him.

She was ambrosia and honey on his tongue. Seductively sweet, and altogether addictive. There was no turning back now, if there ever was before. He felt his cock spurt pre-cum into his briefs and he cursed his own shaky control. With any other woman he would have had no problem staving off his need to be inside her, but with Claudia, the need was like a growing monster in his chest. It consumed all of the oxygen he breathed, and forced him to focus on nothing but sinking into her sweet heaven.

The clamping down of her pussy muscles on his tongue, and the sweet gush of moisture flooding his taste buds, drew a growling sound out of his throat making her shiver underneath him.

"Now!" she whimpered, pleading with him for mercy, and giving him exactly what he craved. Her desire.

Surging to his knees, he opened his jeans and shoved the denim and the now damp fabric of his briefs over his hips, twisting to push them and his boots off before he rose over her on the couch. Her pale skin looked pearlescent against the dark purple fabric of the sofa underneath her, and his cock twitched in his hand.

Rubbing the sensitive crown through the scorching juice between her labia lips, he hissed out a breath of satisfaction as he sunk into her tight pussy. He only made it half way on the first thrust, but a couple of tries later he was balls deep inside of heaven and thanking whatever Gods had brought this woman into his life.

She clung to him, her hands gripping his biceps, and clawing at his shoulders, as she whimpered and moaned her pleasure. The noises drove him harder and deeper. Her legs lifted to wrap tightly around his hips, and he palmed the softness of her ass as she clenched and unclenched those muscles with each thrust.

Just before his balls tightened and exploded he took possession of her mouth again, and drove his pubic bone against her clit firmly, triggering her orgasm. They shattered together, mouths absorbing each other's screams and pants, breathing each other's air as they fell back to Earth.

~ ~ ~

Claudia had only experienced magic like this with one other man, and it stung her soul that she had just betrayed him. How would Mack feel if he knew his own brother was screwing her just two days after their tryst?

Fighting to regain control over her limp muscles, she wiggled underneath the heavy weight of Ryker's body. She wasn't ready to think about the comforting heat of him, or the sweet way he held her to his chest, while still bracing most of his bulk with one beefy arm. Somehow the two Thompson brothers had taken control of her senses, and she didn't like being so off kilter all the time.

There was no future here with them as a unit. They had both made it very clear, and she was fooling herself—or maybe blinding herself with lust. Planting both hands against Ryker's chest, she pushed him off her.

"Easy, love. No reason to move just yet. I kind of like it where I'm at," he grumbled, burying his face in her hair and inhaling. He seemed to do that a lot around her. Like he was an animal imprinting her scent for recognition later. "Why a purple couch, duchess? Of all the colors in the world, why purple?"

"It brightens up the room, makes me smile when I see it. I don't need any other reason. And I need to get up. There's going to be a wet spot on my sofa, and I need to get it cleaned up quickly before it stains. I don't want to explain it if I have to have it reupholstered."

Her tone seemed to click in his brain, and he lifted away from her, watching her warily. A wrinkle marred his perfect brow and his blue-gray eyes looked almost scared of her. "We wouldn't want that. I would have moved this to the floor if I had known how important the couch was to you."

Standing, her weakened leg muscles swayed for just a moment before she was able to take a step forward and away from him. "No problem. Neither of us was thinking clearly. I'm going to jump in the shower first. Please lock the door behind you when you leave."

Refusing to look back, she embraced her flight response and made her way upstairs leaving a silent Ryker naked and alone on her sofa. Hopefully by the time she came back he would have gotten the hint and disappeared. It was bad enough she had betrayed the sweetly honest relationship she'd had with Mack, but she couldn't stomach lying to Ryker about how she felt about him right now. She knew that if she told him she didn't want him, he would walk away, but she couldn't do it now. Not when their shared cum spilled down her thighs, and a faint bruise from his teeth adorned her breast. Not now.

CHAPTER TEN

She had a bag packed and she was on the road by eight a.m. the next morning. As she had hoped, when she returned to the living room almost an hour after going upstairs, Ryker was gone. There was no note, and no pleading, just empty lonely silence to solidify her feelings of guilt.

Instead of facing her troubles in Stone River, she fled for Austin, determined to face her troubles there first. They certainly seemed less intimidating in light of her new problems. Being in love with two men never would have crossed her mind as a possibility for her life a week ago, but now she was faced with the prospect of losing them both along with her job.

It was the one thing she hadn't told them when they asked about her next step. She hadn't revealed that her father was a hard-ass about business, and would be gunning for a scapegoat because the project fell through. Sure, he would have a backup plan, but the question was, whether or not she would be the scapegoat of the backup plan.

Walking into his office brought back vivid memories of her childhood. Since she was knee-high she had come and gone from the Schmidt Properties corporate office with a freedom only the boss's daughter was entitled to. Assured in her position and her right to be there, she would smile warmly at the employees and greet the ones she knew by name. Today, though, she walked with her eyes straight ahead, and her hands fisted at her sides. She'd failed her father, and the taste of her failure was as bitter on her tongue as the betrayal still tingling in her pussy from last night.

Gaven Schmidt wasn't an imposing figure. He stood an average five foot ten and his middle was pudgy from the sweets he loved to enjoy between his meals. Balding and jowly, he was certainly not what most people would consider scary, but she saw him through a child's eyes. She heard his commanding presence even if she didn't see it anymore. Within his sharp honey colored eyes he was a lion like predator that very rarely softened into a purring pussy cat. The smile on his face as she stepped through his door did nothing to reassure her, but she forced her feet to move forward anyway.

Taking a seat while he finished his phone conversation, she looked around the familiar space. A wide cherry wood desk dominated the space in front of a ceiling to floor picture window that allowed him to view almost all of downtown Austin from his seat. On the credenza against the wall was an oversized *Keurig* coffee pot she had purchased for him last Christmas. It was surrounded by photos of her and her mother from the last thirty-five years. So many special moments captured, and frozen in time. Her first birthday, cake smeared over her chubby baby cheeks, and crusting in her pale blonde curls, sat next to a photo of her and her mother on a beach in Cabo from just a couple of years ago. It was like looking through a scrapbook of her life, but in each frame she only saw what was missing.

Her father had always been working. Too busy to take a two week trip to Cabo, too much to do to spend a Tuesday evening at Bass Concert Hall for her ballet recital. She was the star of the show that year, but the triumph had felt as empty as the seat next to her mother.

The phone clicked into its cradle and she jerked her head around as her father rose to greet her. "Claudia! I was wondering when you would make it back. You look too thin, peanut."

Peanut. A childhood nickname that once grated her nerves, and today only added to the pain of her failure. "I've never been too thin in my life, Daddy. Did you get my email?" She accepted a tight hug from him, and then turned to face him as he took the seat next to her instead of going back behind his desk.

He nodded, and grimaced, "I did. The town doesn't seem to understand the value of investment. I've already placed a call to Mayor Edwards, and I fully intend to bring the issue before the planning board again next month. I think we'll up the ante by throwing in funding for a new school, and possibly some park space. What are your thoughts?"

She sighed, and blinked back tears. "I know I should have been able to convince them. I didn't realize how mired in tradition the townspeople were. They are good people though. They welcomed me into the fold quickly, and they weren't nasty when they voted no, but they were very firm. I don't believe they will accept the Granite Estates project anytime in the near future."

"Hmm. Well that's not the news I was anticipating." His forehead wrinkled and he rubbed his chin in thought. "What moves did you make to convince them?"

"I laid every possible positive outcome on the table. From new tax income, to future growth as a suburb of Austin. They weren't interested. I'm sorry I failed to land my first big project. I'm sorry I failed you."

Surprise filled his eyes, and he shook his head, "Your mother warned me that you were in a mood. You've never failed me, peanut. This is business. Sometimes a project goes through without a hitch, but most times you have to jump a few hurdles." He watched her silently for several seconds, and then let out a huge sigh. Reaching out, he took her hands in his. "I'm afraid it's I who has failed you, Claudia. I've done you a grave disservice if you can even for one moment think I would take my frustration out on my own daughter. Did you think I would attack you for not convincing a small town they wanted to become a big city?"

Tears leaked from her eyes, and ran down her cheeks, and she felt her hands trembling in his grip. "I don't know. I guess. I just wanted to seal this deal for you so badly. I wanted you to be proud of me."

"Oh, Claudia, I've never been prouder, but you fight for this company as though your life depends on it, and to tell you the truth it scares me." He rose to his feet and began pacing the room.

She was so shocked that all she could do was stare back at him through teary eyes. "Scares you? Why?"

"Forty years ago when I married your mother I was just starting my own company. Our finances were tight, the bills were big, and I honestly didn't know if I would be able to provide a good life for my new wife. By the time you came along five years later, I had built up a thriving corporation. I was bringing in money hand over fist, and my work became more important to me than anything else. I figured if I paid for every possible lesson and activity, it would help offset the fact I wasn't there for you and your mother. Instead of going to your tumbling practices, I went to business meetings. Instead of watching you win the spelling bee, I went to a board luncheon. I was a terrible father, and I look back now and regret those moments I've lost." He paused in front of the credenza and picked up a photo of her holding the trophy for her first place win in the spelling bee he spoke of.

She didn't even try to hold back her tears now. They streamed down her face unchecked as something inside of her broke open. "You weren't a terrible father. You were trying to give me the best of everything. I had amazing opportunities because of all of the work you did."

"But I taught you that business is more important than the people you love, and that's where I went wrong. I honestly didn't realize it until your mom told me about your phone call."

"She was supposed to keep it private," Claudia grumbled under her breath.

"Well it's a good thing she didn't, peanut. I needed to hear what's going on with you. For months you've had your nose to the grindstone like nothing else in the world mattered. You've become me. It's not a good thing, trust me."

"You're a skilled businessman, Dad, why wouldn't I want to be you?"

"Because being skilled in business has cost me some of the best years with my family, and I can't get them back. Don't ever come into my office thinking I won't love you with every fiber of my being, peanut. I will never see you as an employee. You are my daughter first and foremost."

"But you said this project had to go through when you left me a voicemail," she argued, mystified. For years she had been trying so hard to impress him and win his approval, and she had it all along. It was mind-blowing.

He laughed, "Oh yes, I'm sure I did. I tend to get a little carried away when I'm in work mode. Claudia, you've been working here since college, you've devoted almost ten years of your life to the company. You started from the bottom and you have worked your way to the top. How could you think I would be upset with you for one project falling through?"

"It was important. I was going to prove I was worthy to hand the reins over to," she said in a small voice.

Her father remained silent for several moments. "Do you remember when you were in college, and you mentioned you wanted to be an artist, what I said?"

Claudia grasped at the faint memory. Dinner at her parent's house, an explanation of her current classes, and then a side mention of her hobby, but her father hadn't seemed to take notice, or had he? "No, I don't remember."

Sighing heavily, Gaven leaned back against his desk and shook his head, "I told you to do what you were passionate about, because—"

"Passion breeds success," she finished for him, hearing the words again in her head, and in a new light. "You didn't want me to follow you into the business?"

"Whoa! I never said that. I just wanted you to find something you loved, and embrace it. You tried every possible hobby as a child, but you weren't passionate about them. They didn't feed your soul. If buying and selling properties does that for you, then I will gladly pass the baton to you, but I don't think it does. I know you have put me on some sort of pedestal in your head, but you need to see my failures and imperfections too, peanut. I chose money and success over my family."

Slowly shaking her head, she frowned, "But, I'm not sure what I'm passionate about."

"You seem awfully keen on the people of Stone River. Was there someone special you left behind?" The accuracy of his question made her gasp and she stared up at him wide-eyed, making him laugh, "Yes, your mother told me you were seeing someone. Two someone's in fact, which I'll admit, threw me for a loop. Tell me about these men who have stolen my daughter's heart."

Panic filled her stomach and she shook her head, "I'm not ready to talk about it yet."

"Okay. But don't cut your mother and me out, peanut. I want a chance to meet them, especially if they bring that spark of fire into your eyes. They've got to be pretty special." The reassuring smile on her father's face made her heart stutter, and she felt guilty about keeping the truth from him.

"There's no future there. They don't want what I want, and I live in Austin."

"Do you really want to be with two men, Claudia? Have you thought through all of the issues that could arise? The legalities—"

"I didn't come here to talk about my relationship, Daddy," she interrupted, unwilling to hear the list of cons for this relationship repeated. They had been on a loop for days in her head, so why revisit the issue. "I need to know what my next assignment is."

Instead of answering her, Gaven stood and moved to the coffee pot to fix himself a cup. The silence in the room was deafening and she began to fidget after a few minutes. "Dad?"

"Stone River is your next assignment, peanut."

Shaking her head, she sighed, "I already told you there's no hope for Granite Estates—"

"Not Granite Estates, Claudia, Stone River. I want you to find your happiness, peanut, even if it means breaking your heart first. You can pack your desk up and head back to Stone River as soon as possible."

Shock and anger filled her as she processed his words. "You're firing me?"

"I wouldn't put it that way. I would say I'm pushing you out of the nest. At thirty-five it's time you stopped worrying about my approval, and started living your life for yourself. Go back to that old farmhouse your mom was telling me you bought, and be happy. Find your passion. You have a trust fund, and I'll call the lawyer as soon as you leave to make sure it's turned over into your name. It will last you decades even if you don't work." Gaven looked back at her calmly, but she felt nothing but betrayal.

"After all of the time and work I've put into this company, you're just kicking me to the curb?"

"No, peanut. I'm letting you live. Maybe you'll realize that this is the best place for you, but you need to go figure it out. I'm sorry for upsetting you, but I love you too much to watch you bury your heart in business like I did for the last forty years."

Now it was her turn to pace the room, and she did so twisting her hands in frustration as she worked through his reasonable responses. "I don't understand. What changed? After four decades of nothing but business, why are you so determined to make me feel something when you never did?"

Turning around to face him, she saw what she hadn't seen before. The broken blood vessels in the whites of his eyes, the stress lining his face and the sickly gray tint his skin had taken on since she left Austin a few weeks before.

"What's wrong, Daddy? And don't try to tell me nothing." Crossing her arms, she waited for the worst.

"I'm getting to old for this. My heart is weak, and the doctor is worried stress will bring on a heart attack in the next couple of years. If that happens I'll be lucky to survive, much less come back to work. I've wasted most of my life building a business, but for what? This company can't keep me alive. It can't give me a new heart, or make me a healthy vigorous young man again. Don't waste your life like I have, Claudia. Promise me you will find what makes you happy. No matter what it is." A tear fell from the corner of his eye, and shock washed over her.

Her father was sick. He was in the twilight of his life, and here she was behaving like a spoiled princess. "I'm sorry, Daddy. I wish I had known."

"Why? So you could coddle me like your mother tries to? Bah! I don't need to be treated like an invalid. I just need to know that if something happens to me, you're going to live on and be happy in your choices. So please, go back to Stone River, and find the young man or men that makes your heart skip a beat. Wrap them around your little finger like you did me thirty-five years ago, and don't let go."

Claudia rushed to her father, embracing him and holding him tight. Crying into his shoulder as he hugged her. Feeling a true bond of love with him for the first time in decades. In that moment she should have told him all about the Thompson brothers. She should have explained her dilemma and why she couldn't go back, but she wasn't willing to risk him getting upset. Instead, she clung to him, and whispered promises she wasn't sure she could keep. Comforted by the fact her father loved her and was proud of her no matter what her future held.

She had wasted so much time believing that her father was all about business, and wouldn't accept her if she followed her heart. Knowing that she had his approval eased her soul, and made the pain of losing Mack and Ryker that much more difficult to absorb.

~ ~ ~

Mack slammed the front door behind him as he entered the cabin Friday after taking off early. The stench of alcohol and depression was so heavy it hung in the air making his stomach turn. Ryker was a broken man, and he didn't know how to fix him. For days Ryk had occupied his chair, drinking beer and staring at the television without really absorbing anything on it. All Mack knew was his brother had managed to successfully seduce Claudia, and in turn she had disappeared. They assumed she went back to Austin, but she wasn't answering her cell phone, so they really had no idea at this point. After days with no answers, Mack was tired of it, and he was determined to find his woman, and bring his brother back to the land of the living.

"Get up," he snapped, kicking the footstool Ryker's legs rested on.

The nasty curl of Ryk's lip said more than words ever could, but he grunted a, "What for?"

"We're taking a road trip to Austin."

Instantly a spark of life lit up his brother's eyes, and Ryker sat up, leaning forward. "You heard from her?"

"Nope, and that's why we're going after her. We know where she works. That will get us started." He stomped into the bathroom to shower before packing an overnight bag.

There was no way to know what Claudia was thinking without going after her and asking her. She still owned the house in Stone River, so she would have to come back eventually, but Mack wasn't willing to wait. The more he thought about the half-baked plan he and Ryker had tried to pull on her, the more he felt guilty. If she believed she had cheated on Mack with his brother she would be sick with guilt, and thanks to his brother's silent treatment, he really didn't know if Ryker had managed to tell her they both wanted her or not.

The urge to punch something ran hot under his skin, and just grew more intense when he found Ryker still slumped in his recliner. "What the fuck are you doing? I said we're going after her."

"No, you're going after her. I'm staying here so you can get her back. If I go, there's not a chance in hell she'll even speak to you. Face it, man. Sleeping with me disgusted her enough she left town."

Mack rolled his eyes and grabbed his brother's arm, jerking him out of the chair to his feet. "You will not go back to the pity party you just climbed out of, little brother. I saw the look on her face when she was around you. She wanted you as much as she wanted me. There's no doubt in my mind. So find your balls and pack a bag. You're going with me."

When Ryker finally met his eyes, the look on his face was like a punch to Mack's gut. "I can't hear her say it out loud, Mack. If she wants you and not me…I just don't know what I'll do."

"Don't count the chickens till they hatch, little bro. Get a move on." He forced back his own doubts in order to solidify his brother, and get them out the door. There were no answers until they found Claudia.

~ ~ ~

This was insane, Ryker thought as they walked into the towering building that held Schmidt Properties two hours later. His palms were sweating and his stomach was churning. Claudia might tell them both to go to hell, or she might have them arrested for stalking. What if she hated him after the other night?

He had known the moment she pushed him away something was wrong, but the ache in his heart at her withdrawal kept him from searching her out for answers. When he walked out the door he knew in his heart she had made her choice, and yet here he was chasing after her. It was cracked. There was no way she would welcome them with open arms.

The elevator dinged and the doors opened letting them out onto the floor that held Claudia's office. To their surprise the secretary outside the door explained she no longer worked for the company.

"What do you mean? Did she quit?" Mack snapped at the short round woman who looked a little like a bulldog.

"I'm not at liberty to say, sir, but she doesn't work for Schmidt Properties anymore," Ms. Bulldog responded, shaking her pewter colored bun firmly.

Ryker gave her a flirty smile and relaxed his stance, assuming the role of cocky playboy in the hopes that the good cop routine might bring out her chatty side. "If she's not here, would you happen to know how we might get ahold of her? It's about the Granite Estates project in Stone River, Texas."

Ms. Bulldogs eyes widened, "Oh, of course! I didn't realize you were here on business. My apologies. Mr. Schmidt is on the project until he assigns a new PM to it. His office is up one floor. Would you like me to see if he's available to speak with you?"

Nodding, Ryker gave her a brighter smile, and stroked his beard like he was thinking, "Sure, I suppose that would work. We didn't realize Ms. Schmidt wouldn't be on the project anymore, but I'm sure her father can assist us."

Smiling back at him, Ms. Bulldog rang upstairs and confirmed Gaven Schmidt was indeed in his office and would be happy to speak to the two of them. Once they had reached the safety of the elevator Mack seemed to relax.

"Thanks. I panicked when she said Claudia wasn't here."

Ryker nodded, "I know, but charming women is my area of expertise. You can handle the Papa-bear, since I got Ms. Bulldog."

"Ms. Bulldog?" Mack snickered, "Yeah I can see it."

They exited the elevator and were greeted by another secretary who led them into a well-appointed office. Gaven Schmidt wasn't at all what Ryker expected, and he stared back at the two of them warily.

After shaking their hands, he offered them a seat before saying, "This is an unexpected surprise, and I apologize for the change in project managers—"

"Mr. Schmidt, we didn't come here about Stone River or the project. We're here looking for Claudia," Mack said. His voice was calm and firm, with just enough determination to bring a curious look to Gaven's eyes.

"Claudia? I see. Well, unfortunately my daughter has decided to leave the company and she's currently on a sabbatical. I'll be happy to pass on a message to her, Mr. Thompson, but may I ask why you're so determined to find her?" Gaven leaned back in his chair, and for the first time Ryker saw the vicious shark of a businessman who had built Schmidt Properties into a multi-billion dollar company.

"You can ask," Mack said shortly.

"Please, indulge me. This is my only daughter we're talking about here."

Before Mack could dig them a deeper hole, Ryker intervened. "Sir, Claudia was dating my brother while she was in Stone River, and she left after a misunderstanding. He was hoping to find her and clear the air. Even if she chooses to stay in Austin, it's important we find her and talk to her."

Gaven Schmidt stared back at them, shrewd intelligence taking in their every movement as he decided whether or not to help them. Ryker didn't even realize he was holding his breath until Gaven nodded.

"She needs a man who's just as stubborn as she is, Mr. Thompson. I'm not going to give you her address, but I'll arrange a meeting."

Mack's smile lit up his face, and Ryker felt the same stupid grin spread over his own cheeks. "Thank you, Mr. Schmidt. We would greatly appreciate it."

"Tomorrow evening. I'll book the private room at *TRIO*. Eight o'clock, boys, don't be late." Gaven stood, signaling the end of their meeting, so they followed his lead and headed for the door, thanking him again. Before they were out the door, he stopped them with one more question. "Have you told her you're both in love with her yet?"

Ryker had to grab onto the door handle to avoid falling over in shock. Love? Was he in love with her? He'd only known her a week. Was it even possible? More shock rippled through his system when Mack winked at him and shook his head.

"Not yet, sir, but we intend to tomorrow night at eight sharp."

Gaven nodded, "Good. She needs her world shaken up just a bit but, boys, if you hurt her, I'll bring the hounds of hell down on your heads."

"Understood, sir, and thank you," Mack responded, pushing Ryker out the door in front of him.

~ ~ ~

Claudia wasn't thrilled to get the message from her father that he wanted her to meet him at *TRIO* for dinner Saturday evening. After four days packing up the rest of her belongings in preparation for transport to Stone River, she was mentally and physically wiped out. She didn't particularly feel hospitable now that she was unemployed and anticipating facing Mack and Ryker again.

Going by the voicemails and text messages she had been deleting from her cell phone, Mack knew about her wild night with Ryker. He didn't sound angry, but it was hard to tell from impersonal messages. If she was in his shoes, she would be livid and heartbroken by the betrayal.

Sliding her feet into a pair of navy blue *Jimmy Choo* heels, she smiled at the brilliant splash of crimson on their soles. There was nothing better than a pair of *Choo's* with a new dress to ease a broken heart. Her dress looked custom, but had actually been a deal she found on the rack. Splurging on shoes made her happy, spending willy-nilly on other things seemed childish, and she loved a good deal. Navy and white fabric lined her curves, and a modest V-neck décolletage with a knee length hemline made the dress elegant but understated. She left her hair down, pulling it away from her eyes with a pair of silver combs adorned with moonstone and crystals. Dressed like this she almost felt normal again, and she lamented the fact that she would rarely have an opportunity to dress up once she was a permanent resident of small town Texas. Perhaps she would leave a few key pieces at her parent's home so she could still indulge when she travelled home.

By the time she made it to the restaurant at the *Four Seasons*, she was running about five minutes late, and her nerves were fluttering. Saying goodbye to her parents was an obvious acceptance of her unemployed state, and since she still didn't know what she was going to do with herself once she got back to Stone River, it left her feeling unsettled.

To her surprise, she was led back to the restaurants private room. Normally reserved for parties larger than two, she was frowning over the oddity when the door swung open and her eyes landed on the two occupants of the room.

Mack's golden curls glinted in the dim candlelight of the room, and he flashed his deep dimples in a sheepish smile at her confusion. Next to him, Ryker looked like a man on the way to his death sentence. His hands were tucked firmly into the pockets of his slacks, and his eyes held the light of apprehension. They were a beautiful sight, and yet seeing them was like a firm kick to the gut.

"Claudia, please don't stop now. Come in and talk to us, sweetheart. You look stunning," Mack said in a pleading tone that stole her voice so she couldn't respond.

Forcing her feet to carry her into the room, she felt it shut behind her, leaving her ensconced in the small room with just the two of them. After several awkward moments, she took a shaky breath and asked, "How are you here? Why are you here?"

"We came for you, duchess," Ryker answered, but he looked away when she tried to meet his eyes. "Your father wouldn't give us your address, but he was willing to arrange a meeting, so here we are."

Shaking her head, she felt her hair brushing across her over-sensitized skin, and she shivered. "I assume my father arranged this, but I don't understand why? I didn't return your phone calls, or messages, Mack, so why chase me to Austin?"

"Because I've fallen in love with you, Claudia." His softly spoken response made her knees buckle, but before she could hit the ground he was there to catch her and help her into a chair. "I wish I had told you before you left, but I never expected you to leave without saying goodbye."

"I slept with your brother. I betrayed you." Her confusion and panic made her bluntly honest, and she cringed when the words left her mouth.

Mack just nodded, ignoring Ryker's hiss of anger. "I know, sweetheart, but what you don't know is I sent him to seduce you."

Shame and guilt were suddenly washed away by fury, and she glared at him, "You did what?"

"This is all my fault, sweetheart. I screwed it all up. I thought if you were interested enough in Ryker to allow him to seduce you, I would have the strength to try a ménage relationship, and if you didn't let him make love to you, then I would know your feelings for me were honest."

"You didn't trust my feelings?" She reached for the glass of water on the table, sipping it through dry lips as she fought to keep the glass steady.

"Not exactly. I guess, I didn't trust my own. I was being selfish, and I'm so sorry, Claudia. The last thing I wanted is to hurt you." He dipped his head, and reached for her hand. "Please forgive me for the dickhead move."

She took several moments to absorb his explanation, but every second brought new questions to mind. Turning to Ryker who had remained almost completely silent through Mack's explanation, she narrowed her eyes, "So you slept with me to prove a point?"

"Fuck no. I slept with you because I wanted you more than I've ever wanted a woman. If Mack hadn't even been in the picture I still would have wanted you, but knowing how much he cared about you made my feelings that much more complicated." He rubbed at his chin, scratching his beard as if to help him think. She could see the turmoil in his eyes, their normally gray-blue color had shifted to the bleak color of storm clouds, and his body was taut with tension.

"You had to sleep with me to know how you felt about me?" she asked.

Again he shook his head, "No. I always knew how I felt about you. I was just hoping after sleeping together you would admit you wanted both of us, and I would have a shot with you."

"So, what now? I'm supposed to choose? Like selecting a main course or a dessert? I'm supposed to just decide which of you I want the most, and the other will gracefully bow out?" her anger spewed from her mouth. The hurt and betrayal she had felt on Mack's behalf before now consumed her own heart as she realized they had played with her emotions.

The two men exchanged a look and shook their heads. "No, duchess. We're asking you to give both of us a shot. We want you to come home with us, and date us both. Not a true ménage in the way the Brooks brothers or the Keegan boys do, but we both want a relationship with you," Ryker's words were icy cold against her bruised heart. They wanted to share her, but they were going to remain selfish about it.

"I seem to recall telling you I wasn't a toy to be passed back and forth. You think you'll be content on a Monday evening knowing it's Mack's night with me, and I'm screaming out my orgasm in his bed, while you sleep alone in yours? And, Mack, you're going to be okay with Ryker and me taking off on a lover's vacation one Friday evening because it's his weekend with me? Like some sort of visitation and custody ruling? Are you kidding me?" Pushing to her feet, she propped her hands on her hips and glared at the two men in front of her, "No thank you, gentleman. You can take your ménage offer and shove it up your ass. I might not be perfect, but I damn well deserve better than that. If you can't play nice then I won't either. I want both of you, or neither of you. If you can't come to grips with the fact that I've fallen in love with the two of you as a set, then stay away from me. Don't call, don't write, and you sure as hell better not show up on my front porch begging for attention and making promises you can't keep."

Her hair flew around her as her temper flared, and she spun on her sexy five inch heels, moving for the door. Mack jumped to his feet to stop her, but she could see Ryker's emotional shut down in his eyes. "Claudia, wait! It's not like that. We love you, but—"

Putting out her hand to stop his words, she sighed, "No. No but. There should never be a "but" when someone loves you. My father told me when I came back, I deserved to have happiness, and live every moment of my life without regrets. Well that means giving up people who are destined to continue hurting me, and if this is all you two can offer, than accept this as goodbye."

"You don't understand!" Mack argued, grabbing her hand, but she shook him off.

"I understand perfectly, and I can't do this."

The door shut silently behind her, or perhaps the blood rushing through her ears was loud enough she didn't notice the added noise. Thankfully a taxi sat near the curb, having just dropped someone off at the restaurant. She hurried into it and managed to bark out the address of her home before the dam burst and the tears began to fall.

CHAPTER ELEVEN

Instead of driving straight home to Stone River, Ryker turned the car toward the Northeast. He figured taking Mack to visit their mom would distract him from what had occurred in Austin, now he just had to hope it didn't backfire on him.

"She won't remember us, so I'm not sure why we even bother coming," Mack grumbled under his breath as they entered the Alzheimer's care facility where their mother lived. It was odd to hear him being so down about anything. Mack was the bright light in the family, Ryker was the turbulent clouds.

"But we remember her, or at least that's what you said last time we drove up here," Ryker argued. He was hurting just as much as Mack. Claudia couldn't have been clearer about her stance on a relationship with them, and now they had to figure out how to let her go.

"I get what you're trying to do, Ryk, but it won't work."

Ryker shrugged, "Well then what's the harm in it? You're the one who tells me all the time that we don't visit her enough."

The potent smell of antiseptic and age stung his nostrils as Ryker led the way down the bland hallway to the plain wood door. *Considering the amount this place costs they should be able to hang some pictures on the walls or something*, he thought. In reality he couldn't care less about the décor. It was the knowledge that his mother was a prisoner here that killed him. She became a prisoner of her own mind years ago, but putting her in a secured facility to protect her had felt like locking the cell door.

"Mama?" he called out, knocking softly and pushing the door open.

She was seated in a wheelchair, staring out the window blankly. The blue eyes that turned to meet his were confused and ringed with deep grooves that age had drawn on her face.

Judy Thompson was a beauty before the Alzheimer's stole her away, but Ryker still remembered the way she used to smile at him when he came home from school. It wasn't uncommon for her to have a plate of Oreos and a large glass of milk waiting for him and Mack. They would all sit at the kitchen table and talk about their day while they ate their snack. By the time their father came home from work, chores would be done and supper would be nearly ready. They were a happy family that supported each other in good times and bad.

Ryker couldn't remember the last time they sat at that kitchen table and ate together, or the last time he shared his daily life with his mother. His most vivid memories now consisted of doctors telling him that his mother would never regain herself, and angry confused words from the woman who had always been his rock, because she didn't remember who she was.

"Hi, Mom. It's Cormac and Ryker come to visit." Mack might have started this journey reluctant, but he quickly took the lead moving to pull out a small chair and take a seat near her wheelchair. "How are you today?"

"The birds built a nest in the attic. We'll need to clean it out before it snows." The words made no sense, and pain filled Ryker's chest. It was clearly not one of her good days.

"You got it, Mama. We'll take care of it," Mack answered, meeting Ryker's gaze with disappointment of his own.

Clearing the lump in his throat, Ryker moved closer and reached out to cover her age spotted hand. "How are you feeling, Mama?"

"Tired today. I need to clean up before Danny gets home. Have you seen my boys? They go to the school a block over. Good boys."

Damn it hurt to hear the absence of reality in her voice. She had no idea who they were, or where she was.

"We're your boys, Mama. It's me, Ryker." He knelt next to her, tears burning his eyes as he searched for any sign of recognition in their blue depths.

"Oh Ryker, yes, he's a little devil he is. Keeps me on my toes. Last week Mrs. Martin called me to tell me he was putting spitballs in Lily Colton's hair. Danny was so disappointed. He had to send poor Ryker to bed without his supper."

Ryker remembered that punishment. He had been angry at his father, thinking he overreacted. Looking back he could see how he deserved far worse. The spitballs had been scattered all throughout Lily's dark brown hair, and it took the teacher a good half an hour to pick them out.

"I remember, Mama. I deserved it."

"My Ryker is going to college to play football. He's going to be a big name someday, you wait and see. I was afraid he would skip college to play that silly game, but no sir, he's a good boy. He's going to study hard so he can help his brother become successful. Cormac needs him."

The heavy silence that followed stole Ryker's breath. That had been the plan fifteen years ago. He knew Mack wanted to build his own business, and needed his brother's business smarts to help him, but Ryker was so focused on being successful himself that he let him down. Guilt burned in his gut. Now he had let Mack down in a whole new arena, and possibly cost him the love of his life.

Jumping to his feet, he headed for the door. It was too painful to hear her reminisce about the past and not know the present. Why stay here and inflict this kind of agony on himself?

"Ryk, wait." Mack's voice caught him as he stepped out the door, and he glanced back, "Please don't run away. I know she doesn't know us, but she's our mother. If this is the fate that we face one day ourselves, I'd like to think that karma will come back to us."

"Do you know my husband Danny?"

Mack turned back to face Judy, leaving Ryker to make his own decision about whether to stay or go. With a sigh of frustration he stepped back into the room and took up residence against the wall out of her line of sight.

"I know Danny," Mack answered, bringing a wide smile to their mother's face.

"Wonderful man. Good father, even better husband. He takes such good care of me. Always worried about my happiness and comfort first. I think he'd rob a bank if I asked him to," she laughed. "He told me once that any man worth his salt would give up his very soul for the woman he loved. I never thought much of it until he died. Did you know he died? Had a heart attack, and died. It broke my heart."

Mack's voice was hoarse when he responded, "I know, Mom. It broke mine too."

"He's waiting for me though. Knows I'm coming to him soon, but he keeps telling me to wait a little longer. Says my boys still need me. Do you know my boys? Cormac and Ryker? They're good boys."

Rising to his feet, Mack brushed a kiss on her cheek, and smiled, "I know them very well, and he's absolutely right, they do need you. We're going to go now, okay?"

"Okay, tell Dottie that I will order one of those ice cream cakes for Danny's birthday when you see her. And bring me back some cucumber seeds from the store, would you? I need to get the garden planted before winter."

"Sure, Mom. Anything you need. I love you."

Silently, Ryker followed his brother out of the hospital decorated prison cell, and back to the truck. Instead of firing up the engine, they both just sat and stared out the front window.

"I'm sorry for letting you down, Mack. I knew you wanted me to come back and help with the business. If I hadn't let celebrity and money go to my head—"

"Don't do that to yourself, Ryk. You did exactly what I would have told you to do if you had asked me. You know, mom's right. Dad would have sold his soul to the devil if it made her happy."

Ryker's lip curled up in a half smile, "Yep."

After another long pause Mack sighed, "I feel that way about Claudia, and I know you do too."

"Yep."

"It's like there's something deep inside of me, something primal, something I was born with that matches her. Like puzzle pieces, you know?"

When Ryker didn't say anything else Mack started the truck and pointed it toward Stone River.

~ ~ ~

For two weeks Ryker and Mack kept their physical distance from Claudia, but every moment of every day Ryker's heart ached for her. He didn't know how to fix what they had messed up because he really wasn't sure how they did it in the first place.

The only positive to come out of the whole mess was the closeness he had found with his brother again. After returning from their disastrous dinner and the painful visit with their mom, Ryker had taken it upon his own shoulders to rebuild Mack's leatherworking business. He'd made trips to every ranch within a hundred miles of Stone River, and he had orders for six custom saddles. It wasn't enough business to sustain them, but it was a huge step in the right direction. The only problem he still faced was Mack's lack of desire.

Last night they fought about it again when Ryker presented the sixth order to him and explained the owner of the Kicking J Ranch might be interested in a dozen more if he liked the work on the first one. That was thousands of dollars' worth of business, and yet Mack had blown it off.

"Give it a chance, Mack. Even if we can't build it back up into a million dollar company, we could at least make enough to support ourselves so you're doing what you love instead of working for someone else."

"What's the point? I can live here at Brooks Pastures in a free house working with horses and just creating in my spare time, and not have the headaches to go along with the business," Mack argued.

"But you won't have the headaches. I will. I'm willing to step up and take control of the sales and bookkeeping, while you just create the product. Don't you miss doing what you love?"

"Of course I miss it, but I don't have the money to invest in it, and if we did grow the business then we would have to track down another leather artist to join us, or God forbid train another one."

Ryker punched the wall, and then glared at his brother, "I'll pay for it, you jackoff. I have enough to get us started, and float us for a while. And if they track down some of my missing money—"

"They aren't going to track down your money. Give up the fight already, Ryk," Mack said.

"Oh that's rich. You've been telling me for almost a year to have hope things would work out, but now you're acting like a scolded child because the woman you love is mad at you."

"She's not just mad at me. She hates us both. We've lost her, and so I don't see any point in all of the work to build a business that would overwhelm us. If the business goes well, we would have to bring on new people, and then it becomes less fun."

"You're telling me you won't try because you're fucking afraid of success? What kind of pussy shit is that?"

"I can't succeed without her, Ryk. It's not worth it."

Instead of fighting for Claudia, Mack had withdrawn like Ryker had never seen in his life. Cormac Thompson was a fighter, so seeing him broken and defeated was a shock.

This morning was the final straw. Mack had actually slept in the barn instead of coming back to the cabin, and when Ryker went in search of him, he found him stinking of alcohol and bitter regret.

"This has to stop, Mack."

Glaring back, Mack just grumbled a garbled, "Fuck you."

"I'm serious. You wouldn't let me waste away in a pity party for one, and I'm not going to let you do it either." Ryker took a seat on a hay bale, watching as Mack took his shirt off and dunked his face in a bucket of icy cold water.

"You never really loved her, did you?" Mack snapped.

Ryker fought to hold his temper in check, "That is the furthest thing from the truth and you know it. I love her more than anything else in the world. Hell, she's the type of woman I would have walked away from football for."

His statement seemed to surprise Mack as much as it surprised him, and they both stared at each other in silence, each man dealing with his own broken heart. Finally Mack dropped onto the hay bale across the barn from him and sighed heavily, "I'm sorry, man. I'm trying to let her go, but damn it, I don't want to. I fucking love that woman. I want to spend the rest of my life with her."

"So if I'm hearing this right, you've both fallen in love with the luscious Claudia. And you aren't claiming her because why?" Sawyer Brooks stepped into the barn, clearly having heard their conversation.

Ryker glared at the cocky cowboy, who was happily ensconced in the perfect marriage. "Because we both want her, and neither of us is willing to walk away."

"Again, I'm still not seeing the problem? Look around you boys, this is the twenty-first century, you don't have to duel at dawn to claim the ladies hand," Sawyer said, snickering at their dilemma.

"We offered to share her, but she didn't go for it," Mack said, dropping his head into his hands. He looked so dejected that Ryker felt guilty for loving Claudia. "We haven't seen her for two weeks."

Sawyer's eyes widened and he let out a long whistle. "You boys are dumber than I thought. Hey, Rogan, Parker! Come here a minute!"

The two older Brooks brothers appeared in the doorway a moment later. While Parker waited silently, Rogan spoke up right away sounding concerned. "What's up? Everything okay?"

"Fuck no it's not. These two dumbasses fucked up with Claudia, and need our help," Sawyer said, giving both Thompson brothers the stink eye. Ryker glared right back, refusing to speak up in defense of his choices.

Quickly, Sawyer explained what he knew to Parker and Rogan who took it all in like Army Generals preparing for battle. Rogan turned his dark eyed gaze on Ryker and bluntly asked, "Do you want her enough to do anything to make her happy?"

Nodding, Ryker sighed, "Anything at this point. Life has been hell without her."

Mack agreed, "We already told her we would give ménage a try, but she freaked out, Rogan. She told us she didn't want to be a toy passed back and forth between us. How the hell are we supposed to share her if she won't let us?"

"What exactly did you offer her?" Parker snarled.

"We were going to work out a schedule—" Ryker started to explain, but the three Brooks brothers in attendance all cursed and looked at him like he had just spit on his daddy's grave. "Well then what should we be offering her?"

"Love," Sawyer said. "Don't you get it? She wants you both. She loves you both. So you both have to be full partners in this relationship with her and with each other."

"Fuck that shit! He's my brother and I'm not gay!"

Parker moved so fast Ryker didn't see his fist move until it connected with his nose. Blood gushed out and pain blurred his vision. "What the hell, man?"

"I don't fuck my brothers, and don't you ever insinuate it again. Sawyer means you two have to act like a team if you want to win this woman. Let me put it in terms you'll understand, you couldn't win a football game with just one man running the ball. You have to have other players to throw it, and block the other team's maneuvers. In a ménage relationship, you have to work together to make her happy, because if she's happy you'll be happy. Get it?"

"So we don't have to share a bed?" Mack asked.

"Not with each other. Or at least, not without her in the middle," Rogan said. "With four of us and Rach, we are forced to take turns, and I know the Keegan boys have to do so as well because there are three of them, but you two would be able to sleep with your woman every night."

"What's the benefit?" Ryker asked, using Mack's alcohol stained t-shirt to staunch the bleeding from his nose.

"There's always someone to talk to. Someone to share good times and bad times with. If I'm stressed out and need some alone time, I know my brothers are going to take care of Rachel while I'm gone. She's happy and she loves us all, that makes me happy," Rogan said.

Sawyer laughed, "And then there's the sex. Have you ever tried double penetration? Dude, you're missing out, and so is she. Just because you're fucking the same woman doesn't mean you're gay. It just means she gets twice the pleasure, and if you're the men I think you are, you'll get off on her getting off."

Mack and Ryker exchanged a look, and Ryker could almost hear his brother's gears turning in his head. "I think we've been going about this all wrong."

"No shit, Sherlock," Sawyer said, cursing when Parker smacked him in the back of the head.

"Thanks, guys." Mack stood, and faced Rogan, "I'm going to need to take a few days off, boss."

"Take as long as you need. This is too important to screw up, Mack. Don't hurt her again. Rachel really likes her, and I know she would be upset if Claudia went back to Austin for good." Rogan gave them both a wave, and he and his brothers left the barn.

"Could you live with that kind of relationship?" Ryker asked him with a frown.

Mack shrugged, "I don't think I could if it was anyone else, but maybe with you as the other guy."

"You know, the only thing that weirds me out is the sex. We're bound to touch somehow, and I'm not keen on waking up to see your naked ass every morning," Ryker said, knowing full well that neither reason was enough to stop him from jumping into this relationship with both feet.

Mack snorted, "Yeah, well if I have to live with your ugly mug in order to land the sweetest woman I've ever tasted, I can manage."

"So now what?" Ryker asked, giving his brother a wry grin.

"Now we go get our woman back." Mack clapped him on the back and they both laughed as they walked out the barn with a new plan.

~ ~ ~

Claudia met Zoey and Rachel for lunch at least twice a week now, and she spent most of her days working on her home and enjoying the freedom from corporate pressure. Her townhome in Austin had already sold, and for more than the asking price. The Granite Estates project had been scrapped, and her father intended to sell off the properties and walk away from Stone River for good. If only she had that kind of brass. Instead she stayed in the same place, just miles from the two men who her heart ached for.

It wasn't so bad when she was busy with a project and didn't let her mind wander, but once the sun set and she was alone, it was overwhelming. Every cell in her body wanted to pick up the phone and call them. She wanted to apologize for her anger, and listen to their side of the story, but one thing kept her from doing it. They had knowingly tricked her into having sex with Ryker to verify her feelings, instead of just asking her.

"Are you going to stay in Stone River for good now?" Zoey asked as they dug into ice cream sundae's after their lunch date. Rachel's real estate company was going to handle the sales of the Granite Estates property, and she had a meeting with a prospective buyer for one, so she had cancelled out of their lunch.

"I don't know if it will be for good, but I'm not going anywhere for now. I love my house, and even though I've already put a lot of work into it, it still needs a lot more before I can sell it for a profit." Claudia let a bite of cookies and cream ice cream sit on her tongue, enjoying the memories flowing through her. Ryker loved the cookies and cream flavor because the cookie bits tasted like Oreos. He had brought her a dish one afternoon while she was working, and tasting it now made the pain of his absence sting.

"I'm glad. It's been great having you here," Zoey said with a smile. "So, have you heard from Thing 1 and Thing 2?"

Claudia snorted out a laugh, "If you mean Mack and Ryker, then no. I told them not to call and they haven't."

"Stupid assholes."

Turning wide eyes on her friend, she asked, "Why? They are just doing what I told them too."

"But any good Dom knows his sub will push him away when she's feeling backed into a corner and hurt. Mack should know better," Zoey's words caught Claudia so off guard she dropped a spoonful of ice cream on her lap.

"Shit! Pass me a napkin, please?" Taking the tiny paper from Zoey, she cleaned herself up and then snapped at her, "How do you know about that? Has Mack been telling everyone I'm a kink freak now?"

"Whoa! Back up! Mack didn't say shit to me. Tanner is my Dom, Claudia, and Rachel is Parker's sub. Didn't he tell you Parker was the one to introduce him to The Cage? I just assumed you and he…" Zoey grimaced and a blush stained her cheeks. "I'm sorry. I thought we were there in our friendship. I won't ask again."

Guilt crept over Claudia, and she shook her head with a sigh, "No I'm the one who should be sorry. I'm just oversensitive about the two of them. Mack and I didn't really have a chance to explore before everything blew up. I don't know that I see him as my Dom, as you call it. I just see him and Ryker as the men who stole my heart and then fought over it."

"They'll come to their senses, Claudia. They probably already have, but you won't let them close enough to tell you."

Shrugging, she sighed, "But what does that mean? Coming to their senses could mean they both agreed they don't want me, or it could mean they are determined to have some sort of custody agreement over me. I don't want to have to worry about spending too much time with one of them, and hurting the other's feelings."

"Tell them."

"Oh I did, I just didn't say it so calmly."

Zoey watched her thoughtfully for a couple of moments before she sat up straighter suddenly, "So tell me, if those two suddenly reappeared and asked your forgiveness, offering you a chance at a real ménage relationship with no stipulations, what would you say?"

"I would say hell has frozen over," Claudia said with a giggle, dropping her spoon into her now empty ice cream cup. "In all honesty I would say yes. I miss them too much to have any other answer. It's like a piece of my soul is missing without them. I don't understand it, but it's the truth."

The wide grin that spread over Zoey's face was the only warning that something was amiss, before two looming shadows spread over the table from behind Claudia. Her heart lurched in her chest, and she gasped when Ryker spoke.

"It's about damn time you came to your senses, duchess. Life's been pretty dull without you around."

She turned, and felt her panties go damp at the sight of them. She knew she should be irritated with Zoey for setting her up, but in all honesty she was glad to know her friend cared enough to do so.

"I'm going to let you three have some alone time. Just do me a favor, boys, and take care with her heart this time. Next time you break it I'm going to tell my men to kick your asses."

Claudia giggled at Zoey's parting threat, but the moment the other woman was gone the laughter dried up in her throat. Mack's eyes were wary instead of warm, and Ryker looked hesitant instead of cocky. What had she done to them with her rejection?

"So I guess you heard, huh?" she whispered.

Both men nodded, and Mack frowned, "Did you mean it?"

"Every word," she responded without hesitation. It was time to face whatever future fate had in store for her, even if it meant they made her choose.

The corners of Mack's mouth curled up into a wicked grin, and he reached for her, pulling her to her feet. "Thank God." Instead of kissing her like she expected, he bent and picked her up, throwing her over his shoulder.

"What the hell?" she gasped, bracing her hands on his lower back as he moved quickly across the street to his waiting truck. Ryker was right behind him and quick to open the door so Mack could deposit her in the front seat.

Ryker jumped in next to her, pushing her into the middle of the seat. Before she could protest, Mack was climbing in on her other side. She jerked her gaze back and forth between the two of them. "What are you doing?"

Laughing, Ryker dropped her purse into her lap, as Mack threw the truck into reverse and took off in the direction of her house, "We're not going to give you a chance to escape us again, sweet cheeks. You just said it out here in front of God and the whole world. You're ours, so buckle-up, buttercup. It's going to be a bumpy ride."

CHAPTER TWELVE

They made it to Claudia's house in record time, and before she could protest, Ryker had her over his shoulder and Mack was rifling through her purse for her keys.

"You could at least talk to me before manhandling me," she griped, feeling slightly bruised and very dizzy from her upside down position.

"Last time we tried to use words you threw them back at us. This time we're not talking. We're going to seduce you into accepting us both as your men," Ryker said, letting her slide down his body until her toes touched the floor, and then ravishing her mouth.

His tongue battled with hers as she drew every ounce of pleasure she possibly could out of the kiss. It was exactly what she had been missing for the last couple of weeks. She hadn't realized exactly how interconnected they were, but now, with him kissing her in front of his older brother, she was on the verge of bursting into tears of relief.

Tearing her mouth away from his, she fought to regain control of her breathing only to have Mack grip her chin and turn her head to face him, "Do you remember when I told you that I need my woman to trust me to make the best decisions for her? This is one of those times. Do you trust me, Claudia?"

His silence seemed odd until she realized he was waiting for her to answer him. When she nodded, he took over where Ryker left off. The combined taste of the two brothers on her tongue made her knees weak, and she heard Ryker chuckle as she went limp against him while she kissed Mack. There was no jealousy or condemnation, just pure pleasure.

When Mack finally broke away from her mouth, she could barely think, much less speak clearly. "Can you walk up the stairs, sweetheart?" he whispered to her, his voice heavy with desire.

When she shook her head no, both men laughed. Ryker lifted her off her feet and instructed her to wrap her legs around his hips. Doing so put her sopping wet pussy in the perfect position to ride his erection and she wiggled against him with a sigh of pleasure.

Mack reached down and picked up a backpack she hadn't noticed before, and then followed them upstairs to her bedroom. Once there, Ryker dropped her on the bed unceremoniously, and she watched wide-eyed as they both quickly removed their shirts and shoes.

Giving her a pointed look, Mack asked, "Why aren't you undressed yet?"

"You're serious?" she instinctively scooted backwards on the bed as he collected something black and soft looking from his bag and then stalked her direction.

"Of course we're serious. This time you're ours to play with. Remember what I said about me needing to have control most of the time? Well, you're about to get an up close and personal look at how the Dominant/submissive relationship works in the bedroom. And before you ask, Ryker tops you, baby. So don't go getting the idea you can boss him around or weasel out of this somehow by playing up to him."

"I-I-wh-what?" she sputtered for a response as she watched Mack's crystal clear blue eyes darken with heat. Reaching the headboard, she froze in her movements as she realized she had nowhere else to run. Did she really want to run? Mack was promising her an experience unlike anything she'd had before, so why wouldn't she embrace it? "Okay, but I'm not calling you Sir."

Mack froze, and Ryker burst into laughter behind him, drawing a smile to his brother's face.

"Deal. Now no more talking. Lay back." His instructions were given in a harsh demanding voice that made her clit tingle so she slumped down on the bed until she was lying flat. "Arms up."

Lifting her arms over her head, she watched as he wrapped the black satin material in his hands around her wrists and then around the wooden headboard. Once her hands were secured he looked over his shoulder to Ryker, "Pass me the gag now."

"Gag? Wait a second!" Panic filled her belly as Ryker retrieved another piece of heavier black material.

Mack held it in his hands in front of her so she could see it. "It's not going to hurt you, and you should be able to make noise around it. You just won't be able to cuss me for what I'm going to do to your sexy body."

"I've read books about this. I know I'm supposed to get a safe word," she argued, bringing another smile to his lips.

Reaching into the pocket of his jeans, he tugged free his truck keys. Pulling a smaller than normal one off the key ring, he slid it into the palm of her tied up hand. "This key is special to me. The unit it unlocks holds all of my tools and gear from Saddle-Up. I should have sold it all when the business collapsed, but I couldn't let go of it. I haven't even opened the unit in more than a year. If we push you too far, you drop it and we'll know. But, Claudia, don't let it go unless you want us to stop everything."

Her heart flipped over in her chest as she stared up at him. His leatherwork was precious to him. Letting go of this key would be like letting go of him, and the look in his eyes assured her he knew she would never drop it. Nodding to him, she opened her mouth so he could slide the black fabric in easily. Once it was secured behind her head, he bent and kissed her forehead.

"Are you sure that's a good idea, Mack? I certainly can think of better things to put in her mouth if you just don't want her to talk," Ryker said, winking at her as he adjusted his hard cock behind his zipper.

"This is about teaching her she can trust us, Ryk. Until today we've let her have control of this relationship. It's been about what she feels comfortable with, but now, we're going to make her uncomfortable so she lets us in as her men." Mack stared into her eyes as he spoke, and Claudia felt tears burn the back of her eyelids.

He had to know how uncomfortable she was already. She had never slept with two men at the same time, and she had never delved into the world of Dominance and submission. Part of her was afraid of losing herself if she submitted completely, and part of her wanted to be defiant just to see how far he would push her.

Ryker joined her on the bed as Mack retrieved his backpack and started removing items from it. Drawing out a pair of scissors, Ryker began cutting away the clothes she had never removed. Glaring at him as hard as she could only seemed to make him smile wider as he tore away the last remnants of her armor and left her naked for both of them.

While she was distracted by Ryker, Mack had removed a slim vibrator, a pair of pinchers of some sort, a bottle of lube, several more pieces of satin, and a small butt plug from his bag of tricks. Eyes wide with anxiety, she waited to see what he would do first.

To her shock, he slid into the bed on her other side, opposite Ryker, and the two men began to stroke and fondle her everywhere. Four hands can do a lot of damage to a woman's willpower when used correctly, and she rapidly fell under their spell.

They each touched her very differently, Mack's touch was controlled and firm, he took what he wanted, and gave pleasure in return. Ryker's touch was a soft caress, almost reverent in nature, and as he touched her he couldn't seem to keep from whispering his lecherous thoughts to her. Before long she was writhing under their hands, and neither of them had touched her hungry pussy yet. Every inch of her skin was electrified, sizzling as they stroked her, but she couldn't beg them to fuck her, or even to give her an orgasm, because of the stupid gag.

Biting down hard, she envisioned herself hulking out on them and biting through it, and a choked laugh escaped her throat. Both men stopped what they were doing.

"You're laughing? Did one of us tickle you?" Mack asked, frowning at her when she shook her head no. "Then we need to make sure you have nothing to laugh about."

"Uh oh, duchess. I think you're in trouble now," Ryker teased as Mack picked up the pincher looking things and reached for her breasts.

Instantly she understood what he was doing and began twisting away from him, using her feet as leverage to wiggle out from under his hands. A sharp slap to her swollen tit stung all the way to her toes and she froze mid motion giving him time to clip one of the nipple clamps on. The tips were rubber covered, but it still hurt, and she whimpered when he tightened it just a bit.

"These are beginner clamps, sweetheart. You can take them."

Ryker's eyes were huge as he took in her plump nipples squeezed tight by the clamps. "Fuck. That looks like it hurts." She was going to nod her agreement, but realized he was speaking out of genuine concern, so she shook her head at him. "It looks hot as hell. It's making your nipples a deep cherry red color that makes my mouth water."

Her pussy clenched at his obvious desire, and she saw Mack's face light up in a smile. "If you like that, then you'll love this."

He took a chain, and clipped it onto both clamps and then tugged just a bit, sending lightening through her breasts. Her back arched and she yelped behind the gag. It hurt, but for some reason the pain quickly turned into warm heat making her ache for more.

"Now that's pretty. Flip her over, Ryk," Mack instructed, and Ryker moved to roll her onto her stomach. Mack grabbed her hips and lifted her up onto her knees. The chain dangled and gravity tugged her clamped nipples down sharply. "Look at this, Ryker. She's got the perfect ass for spanking."

Both men were behind her now, and all she could see was the satin wrapped around her wrists and the pillow under her elbows. Every movement made her tits swing like a pendulum and the clamps and chain sent fire rushing through her veins. In her mind's eye she could see herself on her knees in front of both guys as they viewed her wide ass, and dribbling pussy. A flush of shame rushed through her and she dropped her head onto her forearms.

A sharp tug at her hair pulled her back up, and suddenly Mack was in her face checking her hand for the key. It was still snug in her palm, but he noticed the red tint to her cheeks and frowned. "Don't be embarrassed, sweetheart. Ryker and I both love everything about your body. Your response to the clamps makes my balls ache, and I'm looking forward to sinking my cock into your ass after I spank it to a pretty pink color."

She should have been more surprised, but instead she realized she was turned on. Relaxing, she nodded and cocked her hips to present her ass for him. The pleasure in his eyes made her glad she chose that route. Before Mack could move back to his place behind her, a heavy palm landed on the curve of her ass, making her jump.

"You should see how good my handprint looks on your ass, duchess. I think we should consider a tattoo," he said as he ran his hand soothingly over the stinging skin.

Grunting her disapproval, she clenched her ass under his hand. Mack pinched the soft inside of her thigh. "Don't worry, baby, he'll get your handprint tattooed on his ass before I'll let him tattoo your perfect skin."

Soft lips kissed her tailbone, and another hand came down on the opposite cheek. "He's right though, your ass looks as pretty as I expected it to with handprints on it."

A buzzing sound filled the air at the same time as her ass was slapped again. It was hard to focus when so many things were happening at once. One of them slid the buzzing vibrator between her legs to skim over her swollen clit, and she screamed behind the gag. If it weren't for the ties holding her in place she would have shot off the bed entirely.

"I think she's ready now," Ryker said huskily, but Mack just laughed.

"Oh no, she's far from ready. She's going to come a couple of times so there's no chance she'll forget who she belongs to. Why don't you taste her pussy first, while I'm stretching her ass," Mack directed.

She clenched without thinking and suffered another sharp pinch to her inner thigh. Distracted with cursing Mack, she let out a growl of pleasure when Ryker crawled underneath her and positioned his face in perfect alignment with her slit. She let her legs spread a bit, sinking down on his teasing tongue, as she sighed with relief.

The finger pushing into her anus was unexpected, but not unpleasant. It stung, but no more than the clamps on her nipples, and she had tried anal sex a few times in her life. She knew fighting or resisting the intrusion would just make it uncomfortable, so she forced herself to relax. Ryker's swift tongue thrusting in and out of her pussy made that particular task a little easier.

She felt the rising swell of her impending climax as Mack continued to stretch her tight ass, and Ryker feasted on her pussy flesh. Dreading the end of the buildup, she fought it for as long as she could. When Mack realized what she was doing he jammed another finger in her ass and reached underneath her to tug at the dangling chain. Just like plucking a string on a harp, she burst in a crescendo of sensations. Her pussy gushed onto Ryker's waiting face, but he didn't slow his wicked tongue, and before she knew it she was shifting away from his searching mouth because her clit was so sensitive.

"That was beautiful, Claudia. Now we're going to switch places and I'm going to get to taste you while Ryker fucks you with a plug," Mack talked through the steps calmly, and she wondered if he did it just to ease her nerves. He seemed to be very deliberate in his motions, and it warmed her to the core that he cared about how she was adjusting to everything.

The two men swapped spots, but because Mack's shoulders were a little wider than Ryker's, she found herself feeling even more exposed. Mack didn't just tease and torment with his tongue. He used teeth and fingers, and even his nose nudged at her tender clit.

To her side, she felt Ryker's hesitancy as he diddled her ass, and stroked his hands up and down her back. She wondered silently if it was because he didn't want to fuck her ass, or if it was because Mack was sucking her clit right underneath of where he worked. She didn't even realize she had tensed up until Mack paused in his torment and grumbled.

"If you're not going to enjoy this, sweetheart, I can get out a few other toys to keep you focused on pain if not pleasure."

Shoving her knees as wide as possible, she pushed her cunt down onto his face and tried to focus on him instead of her own self-doubts. Ryker seemed to have been jarred out of his hesitation by Mack's comment, and he was rubbing the plastic butt plug against her tiny opening, teasing her with it.

"You have a beautiful ass, duchess. So perfectly shaped, and this tiny pink hole makes me ache. I can't wait to see how hot it is when I sink my cock in it," he murmured as he pushed the tip of the plug past her tight muscles. She whimpered but pushed back on it, until the widest part popped into place and she absorbed the overwhelmingly full feeling it caused. "Oh God, I wish you could see how perfect this looks, Claudia. Your body just opened up for me, and swallowed the plug like a champ. Fuck this, Mack. I can't take this much longer."

Mack's responding chuckle against her sensitive pussy, and Ryker's dirty talk, sent her over the edge of reason again and she bucked on top of him as she came into his mouth. Her jaws were aching from biting down on the gag so hard, and her body was completely limp with exhaustion when he moved out from underneath her. She could feel the ripples of her inner muscles gripping the plug and spasming to hold it close.

When her gag suddenly loosened and fell free, she let out a sigh of relief, and licked her dry lips. Mack pressed a kiss to her temple as he released her arms, turning her gently onto her back, and reaching for the nipple clamps. "This is going to hurt more coming off than it did going on, sweetheart."

Tears suddenly filled her eyes and she fought to hold them back. "So that's it then?"

He jerked on the chain, and Ryker let out a growl as he moved in on her other side, "What are you talking about, duchess? We're far from finished." He grabbed his denim covered cock straining behind his snug jeans, and gestured to Mack's similar state. "Do you really think either one of us is ready to call it quits yet?"

Shaking her head, she managed a small smile before Ryker's lips met hers. He was oh so gentle with her, and she felt hot tears slipping out of her eyes. "Don't cry, lover. We'll take care of you," he whispered as he wiped her tears from her cheeks.

"Claudia, I need to take these clamps off, but you have to brace yourself, because it will hurt, baby." Mack ran his fingertip over the swell of her breast as he waited for her to nod her go ahead. When he tugged the clamp off one nipple she screamed, and a fresh wash of tears poured out of her eyes. She barely noticed the second clamp coming off because pain narrowed her whole world into a red haze.

"Fucking hell! Those are torture devices!" she moaned, reaching to rub at her nipples. Her hands were batted away by the brothers who each took one nipple in their mouth delicately. Kisses, licks, and sweet tender touches eased the burning pain that before long had shifted into a sizzling need in her pussy.

When Mack released her tit, he stood and began removing his jeans. The sight of his thick cock popping free made her whimper with need, and she reached for him, surprised when he held her off.

"If you touch me now, sweetheart, I'll come all over your hand instead of deep inside your ass. Ryker, get your clothes off. Our woman needs your cock."

Lightning fast, Ryker stripped his jeans off and was flat on his back on the bed, moving her on top of him. She braced her hands on his shoulders and lifted her hips to line her pussy up with his hard cock. Smiling up at her, he held it in place, and encouraged her, "That's it, duchess. Right there. Fuck, you feel perfect. I think I'm in heaven."

Full of cock and butt plug, Claudia was feeling the heavenly sensations too, and she heard her own voice pleading with him to fuck her hard and fast. The grimace on his face proved how hard he was struggling to maintain his control. Mack began playing with the butt plug in her ass, his hand holding her firmly astride Ryker's cock. After a few easy thrusts in and out of her anus, he tugged the plug free and set it aside for cleaning.

Rising up over her, she heard him pop open the lube and coat his cock with it.

"This is going to seem like too much, baby, but I promise you can take us both. Do you still have the key?" His hot breath skittered over her ear as he whispered to her, and she nodded, holding out her hand to prove she still held the object in question. "Good. We're going to need it later, because Ryker and I are going into business together. After we finish fucking you into oblivion."

The broad head of his cock pressed into her most private recesses. She tried hard not to fight it, but her body clamped down on both cocks as they stretched muscles that had never been stretched simultaneously. Crying out, she arched her back, trying to ease the pain and the stretch. When it finally stopped, she was gasping for air, fuller than she had ever been in her life, and riding the edge of climax. One little push and she would fall over the edge.

That one push came by way of a thrust from Mack. Followed by a thrust from Ryker, back and forth they see-sawed in and out of her body. Setting off orgasmic ripples that sang in her blood and drew screams from her throat. Heart racing, body swaying, she rode the tidal wave of sensation.

She felt them tighten. She heard them cry out. But she never registered their orgasms because she fainted dead away after her fourth orgasm.

"Do you think we should wake her?"

"No, be quiet. She needs her rest."

Claudia could hear them whispering over her, but she couldn't force her eyes open. Her body was just too tired. Instead she listened to their conversation, relishing the way they sandwiched her in the bed. Waking up every day for the rest of her life would be absolutely perfect.

"That was fucking awesome, Mack. If that's what this BDSM shit is about, I think I need to visit that club of yours."

"Ryker, sex isn't all it's about, but if you're interested we'll set up a time to go. I think Claudia would be intrigued by some of the things available there."

"So how do you think she'll react when we move in here this weekend?"

Trying not to react to the question was particularly difficult, and when she felt their bodies jerking with laughter she cracked one eye open. Both of them were watching her face, and Mack shook his head.

"We knew the instant you woke up, baby. Don't pretend."

Frowning, she tucked her face deeper into Ryker's shoulder and murmured, "Doesn't mean you get to decide when you move in here without me. And since when did you decide to start a business with Ryker?"

Looking pleased, Mack's smile widened, "So you did hear me. I wasn't sure you were still cognitive when I mentioned that. Yes, my little brother has convinced me that with his help in sales and bookkeeping we can rebuild my business. Of course, we could use someone experienced in business marketing to assist us. Know anyone who is interested?"

She winked up at him, and shrugged, "I'll ask around."

"So does this mean we're moving in or not, because I'm sick to death of sleeping on that broken down sofa in the cabin?" Ryker interrupted.

Laughing, Claudia rose up to press a kiss to his mouth. "I love you, Ryker Thompson." Mack sat up behind her, and she twisted to accept a kiss from him too. "And you, Cormac Thompson. I would love to have you both move in here. In fact, I have a whole list of projects I could use your help with, so it will be like having live in handymen."

Her teasing earned her a spanking, and another round of loving, but this time it was gentle and sweet. Instead of staking a claim on her, they were wallowing in their shared love. The future couldn't be predicted, but like her father advised, the only day she could live for was today, and she had a desire to squeeze every drop of happiness out of this life she could.

CHAPTER THIRTEEN

"Sawyer Brooks, you did not just give me a child with a dirty diaper!" Rachel bellowed across the yard at her husband as he darted away from her with a shit-eating grin on his face. "Fuck a duck, that douche-canoe. He's always doing that to me."

Zoey and Claudia both laughed as Rachel carried her giggling toddler toward the house to freshen her up. "My three men better not get any ideas. That won't fly at our house," Zoey said, giving her husbands the stink eye across the picnic table as she rubbed her hand over the tiny pooch of her lower abdomen. They had just announced the surprise pregnancy last weekend, so it was still new and exciting for everyone.

Dalton winked at her, "We've already worked that part out, pretty lady. Clint is getting all of the diaper duties because Tanner and I are too pressed for time to do them."

"What the hell?" Clint hollered, and everyone at the table roared with laughter.

"In all seriousness, Zoey, your men are more likely to fight you for the right to get their hands on the baby. Sawyer's always been a special duck," Rogan said, patting Zoey's hand.

Sawyer waved from the front porch where he was now nuzzling Rachel's neck and stroking their daughter's pretty burnt amber curls to make up for his error. Claudia felt pure joy at the warmth of her friends and family that surrounded her.

Behind her the old farmhouse that once needed a little love, was gleaming with fresh paint from shingles to cellar, and the old maple tree hung over her head, neatly trimmed and waiting for tiny hands and feet to climb to the top. Across the wide yard, Ryker and Mack stood over the barbecue grill animatedly chatting with her father, and the other two Brooks brothers.

The picnic was to celebrate the completed updates on the house, as well as the opening of Tan Your Hyde Leatherworks. Until now all of the orders had been lovingly created in the garage, while Ryker and Claudia turned one of the bedrooms into an office of sorts. When her father found out they were working out of their home, he tried to gift her one of the many empty properties that Schmidt was selling. It was only after Mack threatened to go on strike that she declined the generous offer and purchased the building outright. Now they would have a home for their business, and a home for their new family.

Her eyes dropped back to Zoey's midsection and she felt nauseous. God help her, she wasn't ready for that yet, but having accepted her men's proposal, she was currently also trying to plan a wedding for next spring.

"Claudy?"

Her mother's voice drew her from her thoughts. Linda and Gaven Schmidt had become regular visitors to Stone River ever since their daughter settled in permanently and Gaven's doctor recommended he retire from his position as CEO. They had even begun renovations on one of the Schmidt Properties themselves with the intent of turning it into a place to stay when they visited. Claudia had taken over supervising the renovations on that project as well, against all advice. Perhaps she was taking on too much, but she was passionate about all of her projects.

In that sense, her father had been exactly right. The life she had before wasn't a life. It was an existence that brought her no joy. Spending every night between the two Thompson brothers made her happier than she ever imagined possible, and add in the fact she was doing jobs she enjoyed now, and her life was nearly perfect.

"How are the boys doing, honey?" her mom asked, concern showing in her hazel green eyes. "Did they get everything settled with the nursing home?"

Six weeks ago, Judy Thompson passed away peacefully in her sleep. Two days after meeting her future daughter-in-law. It was a pleasant surprise that she was in a fairly clear mental state that day, and Claudia wished with all her heart that she had gotten more time to know her. Ryker and Mack took it pretty hard, but the three of them had pulled together to support each other.

"Yeah, they got it all straightened out, and all of Judy's stuff was shipped down here. It's still in boxes in the cellar for now. They aren't ready to go through it just yet," she explained. The chill on the breeze harbored the seasonal change from summer to fall, and Claudia couldn't believe how much her life had changed over the summer.

"Give it time."

"I know. They are doing much better now than they were. We've all been too busy to be sad lately," Claudia said with a shrug, sipping the beer in front of her.

"I'm so proud of you, Claudy, and so is your father. You've become the woman we always knew you could be," Linda said, her eyes glistening with unshed emotion.

Blushing because she knew the whole table had heard her mother's endearing comment, Claudia shook her head, "I'm still just me, but those two make me better. I wouldn't be here today if it weren't for them."

Like they were drawn to her by thought alone, Mack and Ryker headed her way with a plate of steaming burgers in hand. "You're the one that's rebuilt us, duchess," Ryker said, planting a sweet kiss on her head. "I was a broken man before you."

"Don't you mean a broke man?" Sawyer asked with a snort that earned him another dirty look from Rachel.

"No, I mean broken. I let my anger over everything with Tina Ash and Scott Weber tear me down, but Claudia here built me back up," Ryker said, stroking her hair gently.

"Uh, I had a part in that too, little bro. You did live with me for almost a year before she came along," Mack said with a grunt.

"Yeah, but she's prettier than you, so I'm giving her the credit."

Laughter echoed through the yard again, and Claudia shook her head at their jokes. "I knew that first night that you two would be the end of Claudia Schmidt—"

"Damn right, duchess! You're going to be Claudia Thompson soon and forevermore. Now, let's eat!" Ryker said to a rousing cheer of happiness from the group. Surrendering her argument, Claudia accepted the fact that without each other, her and her two men would still be bobbing in a sea of despair unsure where to turn for safety. No, they weren't perfect people, but sometimes it took a little polishing to find the diamond under the dirt.

THE END

CHAPTER ONE
BROKEN SURRENDER
SURRENDER SERIES IV

The melodic sound of Blake Shelton's newest country hit, "Lonely Tonight," echoed out the lowered window, and drifted on the soft summer breeze. It was muggy in South Texas, and storms were predicted for later in the afternoon, but at the moment, the sky was a clear blue without a cloud in sight. From where Silas White was parked, he could see the crossing guard helping school children cross the one main road through Stone River. Beside him, his partner, Colby Bruce, snored loudly in his seat. It was a normal day, and he was bored out of his mind.

Just once he'd like to have some excitement. It was part of why he'd become a paramedic—that, and there wasn't much else for a veteran Army medic to do in this part of Texas without more education. When he came back from overseas, he'd had no interest in returning to school just to receive a degree he didn't really want. All he wanted was to help people, and feel necessary in a world that suddenly didn't need him anymore. He missed the adrenaline rush of being on the front lines, but he damn sure didn't miss getting shot at. Hell, in some cases, being the medic was the most dangerous job in the military. He was the one who had to rush to the aid of the injured while bullets whizzed past his ears.

A bee chose that moment to land on the top of his ear, and he knocked it away with a curse. If only he could find something to rev him up. A reason to wake up in the morning that didn't have him chugging back coffee like it was going out of style.

The radio on the dashboard of the ambulance crackled, and Silas surged to life as though he'd been electrocuted. He snatched up the handset before Colby could reach for it, and spoke clearly into it. "Bus 14 to base, we're here. Over."

"Base to 14, call out to 104 Spitz Street. Just outside the apartment, there appears to be a woman injured. The manager wasn't sure what was wrong, but he said she was on the ground next to her car, and she wasn't moving. Over."

"Got it, Deanna. We're on our way." Turning the key in the ignition, Silas eased the large vehicle into the street just as Colby hit the switch for the lights and sirens.

Ahead of them, the school children pointed and waved as they zipped by, and Silas couldn't help but smile. At least someone was excited to see them. Most days, they just sat around doing nothing until the time clock dinged for them to go home, but sometimes they got lucky and got to go to see the kids at the school. That was always fun.

"Wonder what we've got." Colby sat up a bit straighter and fixed his sagging badge on his shirt. "Heart attack? Stroke?"

"Heat exhaustion most likely," Silas said with a laugh.

"Wouldn't surprise me," Colby agreed. "Damned hot even for August."

They turned the corner, approaching the address from the east side, and the late afternoon sun blinded Silas for a moment making him squint to see the apartment building they'd been called to. A low-slung building built back in the seventies, it was one of only three apartment complexes left in Stone River, and this was the cheapest of the bunch. A stranger might assume it was a former motel by the way the doors lined one side, each one with a perfectly matched window next to it, and two parking stalls in front. These tiny apartments weren't meant to hold much, but they were always full.

A blue, two-door car that had obviously seen a lot of miles sat parked in front of the door on the end farthest from them, and a bald man stood near the back end of the car waving his arms around to get their attention.

"Hey Bob, what d'you got for us today?" Silas asked after parking the ambulance, and jumping out. Colby followed with the med bag, and they both hurried to the female now seated on the ground with her back against the hot metal door of the car.

"She just fell over. Like something struck her, but now, she says she's fine." Bob Gunderson owned and managed the tiny apartment building. He was probably one of the nosiest people Silas knew, but at the moment, that might be a good thing.

"Ma'am, can you tell us what happened?" Colby asked.

Silas squatted down next to her, and reached for her, pushing her chin up with his fingers so that he could see her better. When she tipped her head back, he felt like he'd been sucker punched.

"Corporal Bryant?"

"Sergeant White?" Confusion filled her oversized green eyes. "What are you doing here?"

"At the moment, I'm rescuing a damsel in distress," he said playfully, earning a small smile as a reward.

"I'm not in distress. I'm fine. I just fell," she said, avoiding his curiosity by turning her head to watch what Colby was doing.

"That was an awfully strange fall, Miss Bryant," Bob argued. "Looked like you just locked up and then buckled from the middle."

"Did you hurt yourself when you fell, Sarah? Hit your head?" Silas asked, gripping her chin more firmly, this time to hold her head in place while he used his flashlight to check her pupils.

"No, not at all. I bruised my pride more than my ass. I promise you I'm fine." She shook her head, and brushed his hands away, her full lips firming into a tight pout.

Silas exchanged a look with Colby who shrugged his shoulders and proceeded to put away the supplies he'd just removed from the med bag. Something felt off about the way Sarah was responding, and he wasn't buying her no injuries claim. If she'd really just slipped and fallen, why didn't she get back up and brush herself off? Why sit in the hot sun against an equally hot car?

"All right. Well, I can't throw you over my shoulder and haul you to the hospital, but I can offer to help you up and back inside." Silas stood and held his hand out to her.

As expected, she stared at it in horror and shook her head. "I'm fine right here, thanks. You boys can go on about your business."

Planting his hands on his hips, he laughed. "So to avoid telling me what's really wrong, you're going to sit in the gravel with the sun burning you up to a crisp?"

She rolled her eyes and wrinkled her nose. "I'm telling you, I'm fine—"

"Prove it." He waited with his hands on his hips as she considered his challenge. There was fire in her eyes; the woman he knew from years ago could never resist a dare. For just a moment, he thought she was going to launch herself to her feet and punch him in the jaw for being an asshole, but then her eyes dropped and she shook her head sadly.

"I can't." Her words were soft, so he dropped back down beside her, conscious of the way she kept her gaze lowered and the responding twitch of his cock in his pants. Damn, he loved a feisty woman when she submitted.

"Tell me what's going on, Sarah."

He saw her grit her teeth and glance toward Colby and Bob before she hissed, "My back spasmed, and locked up. I just need to sit still for a bit until the muscle relaxer kicks in."

"Muscle relaxer? When did you take it?"

155

"A few minutes ago when Bob brought me a bottle of water. I swear I'll be fine."

He nodded in understanding. "Does this happen a lot? Random back spasms?"

"Too often for my taste," she admitted. Her phone beeped and she dug it out of her purse, wincing when it twisted her upper body.

"You know it's possible you hurt yourself when you fell and didn't realize it because of the spasm." He was determined to get her to at least let him check her over. Even if she refused to go to the hospital, it was clear she wasn't fine.

"Unlikely," she said dismissively, glaring at her phone and then tossing it back into the depths of her purse.

Colby cleared his throat and turned to Bob, distracting him with a question about the choice of paint color on the apartment building, and giving Silas a moment of privacy with Sarah.

"Sergeant White, I realize you want to help, but—"

"Silas." He shifted around to sit next to her, his shoulder pressing against hers, and his back against the scorching hot car. "Damn woman, no wonder your back hurts. You're gonna have third degree burns from sitting here against this metal."

"It wasn't like I picked this spot for the view." she said with a laugh.

"Why won't you let me help you, Sarah?" he asked.

She shook her head. "I don't need help."

"We all need help sometimes."

"Not today," She insisted through clenched teeth. "Look, Sergeant, I know—"

"Damn it, is it so hard for you to call me Silas? I'm not in the Army anymore, Corporal Bryant. You don't have to address me by my rank."

She flushed and wrinkled her cute nose up again. "Old habits die hard, I guess. I know you want to help, but I'm perfectly fine. In a few minutes, the meds will kick in and I will be able to get up and go inside. I'll take a cool shower to ease the sting of the sun, and then lay down for a nap. Okay?"

"Okay," he agreed, crossing his ankles and resting his head against the car behind him.

They sat there for a minute in complete silence before she huffed and asked, "What are you doing?"

"Waiting."

"For what?"

"For your meds to kick in. Once they do, I'll help you inside and check you over for injuries. If you're uninjured, I'll say goodbye and go on about my merry way." He gave her a wide grin when her mouth dropped open.

Her frustration was obvious, but there was no way she was going to convince him to leave her sitting here alone. Corporal Sarah Bryant had been one of the best soldiers he'd had the honor of working with. She was loyal, disciplined, kindhearted, and she made a damn fine soldier. He hadn't spent much time one-on-one with her, because every time he looked her way, his cock twitched in his pants. That kind of reaction didn't usually go over well with the females in his unit. More often than not, it was a direct turn-off. He'd seen too many guys test their luck against the battle-hardened ladies and regret it, so he'd kept himself at a polite distance.

His unit had been sent back home long before hers was scheduled to return, so he had no idea how the rest of her deployment went, but the first half was very rocky. They'd survived hell on Earth and ended up in the same tiny town in Texas. There was no way that was a random coincidence.

"How long have you been back?" he asked.

"Two years."

He felt his eyes widen in surprise. "I thought you guys were going to be there a year?"

"The unit didn't return until the summer of 2013, but I got to MEDEVAC back in January that year."

His heart rate doubled. "What happened?"

"You know, I'm feeling better now. I think I can probably get up and go inside." Just like that, she shut down his question, forcing him to refocus his attention on her injured status. His gut told him that her back pain and her early return home from deployment were related, but if she wasn't ready to explain, he'd let it lie.

"Great. Let me help you so that you don't slip on this gravel. No need getting an injury if you don't have one." He jumped to his feet and reached for her hand, pleased when she let him take it. The skin of her palm was rose-petal-soft against his, and when she slowly stood, the scent of raspberries swirled in the air around her.

Her dark hair was pulled back in a bun at the base of her neck and her comment about old habits ran through his brain. She was right. It was impossible to give up military life completely. The fact that she'd obviously had her time cut short probably made it even harder.

The first step she took was tentative, but once she was assured that her body would hold her up, she smiled. Her beauty was blinding. She was a stunning woman, and she took his breath away. In an attempt to recover his sudden fumble, he bent and retrieved her purse, handing it to her.

"Thanks." She accepted the large bag, and moved carefully across the gravel. To his disappointment, she leaned on the car rather than him, but he was glad to see her moving on her own.

It took a moment for her to find her keys, but once the door clicked open, they were hit in the face with a wave of blissfully icy air from inside the air-conditioned apartment. The same berry scent filled every nook and cranny of the cozy space. Silas breathed it deeply into his lungs, committing it to memory.

He waited near the door as she put her purse away and kicked off her shoes, wincing when her back was twerked in an awkward angle.

"Tell me, did the back spasms start after your vacation in Afghanistan?" he asked.

"Good guess," she said, laughing dryly. "Not the best souvenir, or the best vacation for that matter."

"I'd have to agree. I wanted to bring back a sand spider, but customs wouldn't let me. No animals, vegetables, minerals, or giant insects apparently."

His playful, easy chatter helped her relax, but she still kept her distance. The apartment was miniature compared to the home he and his brother Jeremy lived in. The living room was also the dining room, kitchen, and office with only two doors branching off at the back. He assumed one was the bedroom and one was the bathroom, but he doubted she'd give him a tour.

As much as he hated seeing her cramped into the small space, he was glad to know she had a place. Too many veterans they served with were struggling to find work and keep a roof over their heads.

"Thanks for the help..." she said, her words drifting away as she fidgeted awkwardly. It was clear she wanted him to leave, but he wasn't ready to go yet.

"Anything hurting?"

She shook her head, "Not really. I'm embarrassed more than anything. I tried to tell Bob that I was fine, but he insisted on calling for help. I hate to have wasted your time."

"It's not a waste of time. I got to help a pretty woman and see an old friend. I call that a win-win." He moved slowly across the room, worried that she would feel cornered if he moved too quickly. As he drew close, he saw her swallow hard, and her eyes locked on his lips. The tiny, pink tip of her tongue darted out to wet her own lips, and his cock surged to attention.

As much as he wanted to reach out and see if she was feeling the same attraction, he knew this was not a good moment for it, so he reached for her shoulders and turned her to face him head on. "Lift your arms."

She frowned in confusion and he laughed. "So that I can see if you're hurt. Lift your arms."

She followed Silas' instructions, and he manipulated her arms and shoulders, and then circled to her back. He ran his fingers down her back and felt the tightness in the muscles on either side of her spine. "Have you tried massage therapy?"

She flinched when he hit a particularly tender spot and hissed, "Too sensitive."

"Hmm...with the right physical therapist I would think—"

"It's fine. Some days are better than others, but I'm tough."

He nodded and moved back around to face her. "I never doubted it for a moment. Are you seeing Dr. Keegan?"

"Who?"

"Dalton Keegan is the only doctor practicing in Stone River," he said with a pointed glare. "If you're not being treated by him, then who are you seeing?"

She flushed, and turned away. "A doctor in Austin."

"Who?"

"Are all EMTs this nosey? Seriously, I've proven to you that I'm uninjured and capable of taking care of myself. I appreciate your concern, but I really would like to lie down now." The brush-off irritated him, but he figured in her position, he'd feel the same way. It wasn't her fault he was fighting the urge to keep her close.

"I apologize if I'm coming across as nosey. I just want to make sure you're okay." Reaching into his pocket, he withdrew a card with the phone number for the ambulance company on it. Quickly scribbling his personal cell number on the back, he handed it to her. "Here's my number. If you need any help at all—or if you have another back spasm—don't hesitate to call me."

She snorted and rolled her beautiful eyes. "Right, so you can bring the happy van to visit again? I think not, but thank you anyway."

"No, I'm saying this as a friend. If you need help, call me. In fact, call me even if you don't need help. I'd like to..."—he adjusted his stance as his body responded to his lewd thoughts—"reconnect. It would be nice to talk about old times."

A sad look flitted across her features before she recovered herself and gave him a smile. "I could use a beer with a friend."

Instantly he felt a surge of hope, and he jumped on it. "Tomorrow night? Robin's isn't usually too busy on a Tuesday evening. We can have a beer and catch up."

"Sounds good. Thanks again, Sergeant...er...Silas."

"Anytime, Sarah, anytime."

With that, he left her behind in her small apartment and spent the rest of the day thinking about her. He didn't remember her being so beautiful, but he hadn't been in a position to admire the women he was serving with at the time.

He was also still married when he was deployed.

The day he returned home, his wife served him with divorce papers rather than welcoming him at his coming home ceremony, but he wasn't surprised. Before he left, their marriage was on the rocks, and his deployment just made it worse. They parted as amicably as two people could, and he moved back into his childhood home with his brother.

Turns out he and Jeremy were closer now than they'd been as kids. They had become best friends in the last two years, and recently they'd even tossed around the idea of looking for a different sort of relationship.

Stone River, Texas, was home to several unconventional relationships. There was the Brooks family, which consisted of the four Brooks brothers: Rogan, Parker, Sawyer, and Hudson, along with their wife, Rachel. There were the new residents, a pair of male teachers who were partners in more than just their teaching abilities. Silas had enjoyed a beer with Levi and Quinn once, and they were two of the nicest men he'd ever met. Their arrival had certainly caused a stir when they took the jobs at the local school. A handful of people were uncomfortable with the gay couple teaching their children but most were welcoming. It was as if their small town had its proverbial eyes opened and was now embracing the unconventional. He was genuinely proud to be a resident of Stone River nowadays.

Nevertheless, as much as he liked the idea of finding a special woman to share with his brother, he wasn't so sure that was a real possibility, so he'd continued to date on his own. The question was: How would Jeremy feel if he actually found someone himself?

The image of Sarah Bryant immediately popped into his head. What would Sarah's opinion be of ménage relationships? Not that it mattered, his attraction was most likely one-sided. As gracious as she'd been about going out with him for a beer, he wasn't so sure she would be as easy-going if he told her he wanted the woman in his future to join him and his brother in a relationship.

No, it would most likely be just a casual beer with a friend, and sharing a few dozen memories. No big deal.

Available now at your favorite retailer!

WWW.LORIKINGBOOKS.COM

ALSO BY LORI KING

Crawley Creek Series
Beginnings
Forget Me Knot
Rough Ride Romeo
Claiming His Cowgirl
Sunnyside Up
Hawke's Salvation
Handcuffed by Destiny

Fetish & Fantasy
Watching Sin
Submission Dance
Mistress Hedonism
Masquerade

Surrender Series
Weekend Surrender
Flawless Surrender
Primal Surrender
Broken Surrender
Fantasy Surrender

The Gray Pack Series
Fire of the Wolf
Reflections of the Wolf
Legacy of the Wolf
Dreams of the Wolf
Caress of the Wolf
Honor of the Wolf

Apache Crossing
Sidney's Triple Shot

Sunset Point
Point of Seduction

Tempting Tanner

ABOUT THE AUTHOR

Best-selling author, Lori King, is also a full-time wife and mother of three boys. Although she rarely has time to just enjoy feminine pursuits; at heart she is a hopeless romantic. She spends her days dreaming up Alpha men, and her nights telling their stories. An admitted TV and book junkie, she can be found relaxing with a steamy story, or binging in an entire season of some show online. She gives her parents all the credit for her unique sense of humor and acceptance of all forms of love. There are no two loves alike, but you can love more than one with your whole heart.

With the motto: Live, Laugh, and Love like today is your only chance, she will continue to write as long as you continue to read. Thank you for taking the time to indulge in a good Happily Ever After with her. Find out more about her current projects at http://lorikingbooks.com, or look her up on Facebook: http://www.facebook.com/LoriKingBooks or Twitter: https://twitter.com/LoriKingBooks.

Printed in Great Britain
by Amazon